The Problem You Have

Lynn and Lynda Miller Southwest Fiction Series
LYNN C. MILLER AND LYNDA MILLER, SERIES EDITORS

This series showcases novels, novellas, and story collections that focus on the Southwestern experience. Often underrepresented in American literature, Southwestern voices provide unique and diverse perspectives to readers exploring the region's varied landscapes and communities. Works in the series range from traditional to experimental, with an emphasis on how the landscapes and cultures of this distinct region shape stories and situations and influence the ways in which they are told.

Also available in the Lynn and Lynda Miller Southwest Fiction Series:

The Last Hanging of Ángel Martinez by Kate Niles
Nopalito, Texas: Stories by David Meischen
Hungry Shoes: A Novel by Sue Boggio and Mare Pearl
The Half-White Album by Cynthia J. Sylvester
Girl Flees Circus: A Novel by C. W. Smith

THE
PROBLEM
YOU
HAVE

STORIES

Robert Garner McBrearty

University of New Mexico Press | Albuquerque

Library of Congress Cataloging-in-Publication Data

Names: McBrearty, Robert, author.
Title: The problem you have: stories / Robert Garner McBrearty.
Description: Albuquerque: University of New Mexico Press, 2025. |
Series: Lynn and Linda Miller Southwest Fiction Series
Identifiers: LCCN 2024032521 (print) | LCCN 2024032522 (ebook) |
ISBN 9780826367730 (paperback) | ISBN 9780826367747 (epub)
Subjects: LCGFT: Short stories.
Classification: LCC PS3563.C33358 P76 2025 (print) | LCC PS3563.
C33358 (ebook) | DDC 813/.54—dc23/eng/20240712
LC record available at https://lccn.loc.gov/2024032521
LC ebook record available at https://lccn.loc.gov/2024032522

Founded in 1889, the University of New Mexico sits on the traditional homelands of the Pueblo of Sandia. The original peoples of
New Mexico—Pueblo, Navajo, and Apache—since time immemo-
rial have deep connections to the land and have made significant
contributions to the broader community statewide. We honor the
land itself and those who remain stewards of this land throughout
the generations and also acknowledge our committed relationship
to Indigenous peoples. We gratefully recognize our history.

Cover illustration by Fons Heijnsbroek on Unsplash
Designed by Felicia Cedillos
Composed in Chaparral Pro

As ever, to Mary Ellen and our sons, Zane and Ian, and to all my friends and family

Contents

Acknowledgments

Grateful acknowledgment is given to the publications in which some of these stories first appeared: *Fiction*, "Heading for Shore"; *The Missouri Review*, "A Morning Swim"; *Witness*, "Sarge and Hollings"; *The North American Review*, "Convergence," "Cold Night in Waterloo," and "Episode"; *The Greensboro Review*, "Holdouts"; *Green Hills Literary Lantern*, "The Professor's March"; *Narrative*, "Teach Us"; and *Pocol Press*, "The Bike."

I would like to thank my editor Elise McHugh for her warm encouragement and guidance, and all the great team at University of New Mexico Press for making this collection possible. I would also like to thank the various editors who first published some of these stories, in particular Grant Tracey at *North American Review* and Speer Morgan and Evelyn Somers at *The Missouri Review*. I am also deeply grateful to a variety of fellow writers, editors, teachers, friends, and organizations that have been supportive of my writing over many years, including Jack Smith, Barry Kitterman, Tim Hillmer, Tom Lamarr Jones, David Wroblewski and Kimberly McClintock, Jim Jamieson, Dick and Debbie Stein, Robert Lunday, Phil Brady, David Kysilko, Michael Mewshaw, Don Eron, Sigman Byrd, Kerry Reilly, Steve Wingate, Mark and Ruth Brown, Steve Arney and Virginia Schultz, Chris Schweitzer and Karima Thobani, Nick and Diane Rehnberg, Don and Donna Thompson, Cathy Schueler, Mitzi Mabe, Caleb Seeling, Stories on Stage, The Western Touring Society, and to many other friends not named here. As ever, I am grateful to my beloved Mary Ellen and to our sons, Zane and Ian; to my delightful siblings, Gerald, Kevin, Mary Ella, Steve; to my nephews, nieces, brothers- and sisters-in-law; and to those I hold in loving memory, including my parents and my sweet and brilliant niece Shauna.

One does not exactly write a collection of stories but individual stories which eventually call to be collected into a book. One ponders which stories to include, which ones to leave out. As I contemplated these stories various themes suggested a certain cohesion, in particular themes concerning turning points, choices, doing the right action or not, or being uncertain about the right course of action. At the same time I was glad, as various early readers mentioned, that there was a diversity of characters, from the old to the young, people on the run from the law to people leading seemingly stable lives. Whatever their circumstances, the characters are haunted by a curious inner call to make a change for the better, whether they always heed that call or not. I am grateful and delighted that University of New Mexico Press has chosen to publish these stories.

COLD NIGHT IN WATERLOO

SOMEWHERE OUT ON THIS country road, Paul comes to, freezing. The cold is sobering him up fast now, and it wasn't a complete blackout this time, but he knows with regret that for the last few minutes he was functioning in that otherworldly state he knows too well, and damn, he blew a ride in a warm car with three guys and a girl he hooked up with in the honky-tonk bar just outside his cheap motel on the highway. They thought he was funny at first, all of them bump-dancing with their butts, and he thought the girl, skinny and dark haired, with gleaming teeth, might be a little sweet on him, might be seriously thinking of dumping the duds she was with, which led him to make that stupid pass in the car at her when they invited him to go to a party outside of town. He has a fuzzy memory now, crammed up against her in the backseat, leaning in and blowing in her ear. Had he really said, "Let's light it up, baby, let's light it up tonight. What do you say, you and me?" What the hell sort of thing was that to say to a girl? That was a stupid thing to say, like out of a bad movie.

At thirty he seems to be doing that more and more, playing characters in bad movies. It's been one bad roll after another since getting out of the service. Holding himself, hugging himself, now using his hands to beat a little heat in around his chest—he's got a cheap parka, not worth a crap in this near zero weather—he remembers he didn't just whisper to her; he touched her thigh until he felt the warmth beneath her blue jeans. But then she blew a hard breath, grabbed his hand and threw it off her like something diseased, and yelled, "Oh, God! He's *touching* me! Get him out! Get him out of the car!"

The driver pulled to the side of the road. "Get out, you asshole." The guy in the back seat over against the other door reached past the girl to slug him, punching him over her shoulders so the punches were bouncing off his head, little dings that he could ignore, but then the other guy in the passenger seat got into it too, turning around in the seat and punching at his forehead, more annoying dings, and he thought about kicking their asses and making off with the car and the girl.

But, politely, keeping his cool, he said, "Okay, okay, I'm going. Fuck you all if you can't take a joke." Out he went and they peeled off, and here he is in the dark, freezing his ass off, his cell phone dead—forgot to charge the goddamn battery. *Oh, God!* What did she mean by wailing out like that, like he was some kind of monster?

What he needs right now, goddamn it, there it is. The one thing he needs most in the world is that farmhouse, that porch light shining back from the road a hundred yards ahead and down a long gravel driveway. He's going there. People who live in places like that, maybe not even working farms, but a little land, grow a few tomatoes or something, those people are the salt of the earth, read the Bible, don't turn out the stranger in your midst. Won't let a guy freeze.

Not another place in sight. Pickup truck in the driveway. Solid folk, kindly people.

He walks up the wooden steps of the porch; off to the left, a swinging bench—*salt of the earth!* He pauses a moment in the yellow porch light of the old white house with the chipped siding. Knocks. Knocks louder, hugging himself. He's got to get in. He's got to get out of the cold. He's not dying out here. *Nobody's dying tonight, not happening, not on my watch.*

A dog, a fierce brute, from the sound, letting loose inside. He likes dogs, but this pup doesn't sound friendly. A door opening, stopped by a chain lock, and an old man peering through the crack. The dog, a German Shepherd, barking to kill. The old man swats at the dog. "Shut up, Claude." The dog whines, but he's pushing his nose past the man's leg. "What do you want?' Paul hears noise, people talking in the background. That could be good. Old guy will be less afraid if he's not alone. But the sound changes and he realizes it's only noise from the television set back in another room.

"My car broke down. A mile from here, a couple of miles from here. I've been walking. I'm sorry to bother you, mister. I'm freezing out here. It's cold as . . . it's cold."

The old man's eyes glint behind glasses—sharp little eyes—and the white, thin eyebrows give the old bird a harsh sort of look. "Why are you out on this road? Where are you from?"

"I'm just passing through. I was trying to get to this party."

"A party? There's no party out here, son."

"Yeah, well, it was all kind of a big misunderstanding. I'm just trying to get back to town. I got a motel room there."

The old man nods slowly. "I'll call somebody for you. You give me a number to call."

"I'm not from around here. I don't have anyone to call." One good kick might break that chain, drive the door in, but there's the dog. It bares its teeth and growls before the old man swats him again. "Shut up, Claude. That's enough. I'm trying to talk to the man here."

Trying to talk to the man here sounds good; willing to work with a guy, salt of the earth. If he does kick in the door, the man might take it the wrong way, will think he'll hurt him when he just needs to get out of the cold.

"Tell you what, son, I'm going to call the sheriff to come by and give you a lift to town. He lives just a couple of miles from here, or he'll send the deputy. Won't take long." The old man says *sheriff* and *deputy* in a way he knows will drive him off.

Paul stares at him through the crack. "Never mind, mister. I'm moving on. I'll just freeze to fucking death out here. You remember that." He falls backs from the door as if tugged away and heads back down the gravel driveway, but once out of the circle of light cast by the porch light he's in the darkness. And there's the pickup truck in the driveway. He's hot-wired cars a couple of times, but he wasn't that good at it, and that was in the light. In the dark, with his frozen hands, that's not going to work. There's a shed. He could hide out in that, pull some sacks over himself or something. But the shed's padlocked.

There's that barking again, but louder. The old man might turn the killer dog loose to make sure he clears out of here. Let a guy freeze out here—ought to die on his doorstep, make him happy. He's never imagined how great a cheap motel room could be. Just the warmth of that room would just be so great right now. Why did he get in this fix, all over a girl who had the best teeth in the world? He can see that smile now; it lit up that barroom. She probably did have a thing for him. He just moved a little too fast.

They don't usually lock the windows in these old farmhouses. He picks a window in the back, in the far corner of the house. The piled-up snow gives him a good cushion, raises him to the right level. Perfect. Not even a screen. Sure enough, the window jams up, then releases. He pushes the window higher, gives a hop, lies sprawled in the frame. He drops into a dark room. He crawls his way along a carpeted floor. The old man cries out from the front door, "Claude! Claude! Come back here, you stupid dog!"

Claude's clueless. His barking recedes into the distance, down the country road, maybe out on a long romp after some dog buddy or girl. Good to get old Claude out of the picture. Paul lies on the floor, breathing. Okay, he knows this scene. Scenes like it. Plenty of dark houses he's gone into. But that's with a flashlight, though you didn't want to use it much—as little as possible. And not houses with people inside. At least not intentionally, though he'd been surprised a couple of times. Now he's got an old guy loose in the house somewhere. He doesn't think there's anybody else. The guy's too old to have kids living with him, and if there was a wife, he'd have heard something from her by now. He could just bed down in this room, just stay on the floor, but that's risky. Doesn't know if the old man is going to get suspicious and prowl around. The old buzzard might have already called the cops. But he can't head back out to freeze. The keys. Okay, he's got to find the keys to the truck and get out of here fast. He remembers that on the drive with the three losers and the girl with the gleaming teeth—maybe it wasn't too late, he'd find that party and pull up in the truck and off they'd go—they'd passed branch roads. Avoid the cops, who'd be thinking he was some sort of dumbshit who'd panic and head for the highway. Hit those back roads instead and work his way around to the motel, exchange the old truck for his own car and get out of town. They'll be looking for the truck, not his old beater. He can still get out of this one.

But find those keys. Find those keys fast. He rises to his feet. Creeps down a hallway, eyes adjusting now. *Remember your strengths! This is what you're good at! You are very damn good at this! Then why have I always hit half-ass houses? Why not a high-rise now and then? I'm getting out of it, I'm getting out of the field, the field's moved on. I didn't want to do this. This is the last time . . .* He moves toward the light of the den. He hears the TV again and the old man is probably sitting there watching *Hawaii Five-O*, probably never called the cops at all. *Maybe I'll just walk right in and say give me the fucking keys. No, be nice. Don't give him a stroke.*

Sure, he knows how these houses work. These rooms off the hallway are where the kids used to live, but they're empty now. Then there'll be a little living room, the front door off to the right, a den with the TV to the left—probably some old TV with a yellow screen, hardly worth ten bucks at a pawn shop. Another room off the living room where the old man sleeps. Lonely old guy. Wife probably died. Should say something consoling to him. His own mom had died, and dad too. They were good people. He hated it when people blamed their parents for how they turned out. His parents had been good people! He wouldn't have anybody speaking out against them! The TV turns off suddenly. That could be good, old guy going to bed. He freezes in the hallway, listens. Okay, go, easy.

Into the living room now, keys probably hung up right by the front door. Yes, that's where he'd keep them, that's where they always keep them in farmhouses.

Crossing the hardwood floor toward the keys, his heart lurches and he halts abruptly. The old guy is standing behind an armchair staring right at him, and worse, a whole hell of a lot worse, is that the old man is aiming a shotgun right at his chest.

"Stop right there," the old man says.

"Okay," Paul says. "Okay. Don't shoot. I don't mean any harm."

He goes all weak inside, legs trembly. Nothing worse than a shotgun at close range. Looks like he know how to use it too. Probably some old marine. That gun will blow him in two if the man's finger goes all twitchy.

The chair is a nice touch. A good, smart touch. Keeps him from lunging at the old man, if he even wanted to.

"You stand right there."

"Yes, sir."

The old man squints. "No. Sit on the floor."

He starts to obey, then shakes his head. "No."

Louder now, a wag of the gun, but a waver in the man's voice. "Sit on the floor."

He had to know this. He knows now the old man won't shoot easily.

"I'm going to leave. I'm going to walk out the front door."

"Don't move."

"I'll walk out of here. You don't want to shoot a man in the back. The cops will pick me up."

He sees something change in the man's face. Maybe the old guy hasn't called the cops after all; maybe heard a noise and picked up the shotgun first.

"Okay. Go ahead and walk out of here."

"I wasn't going to hurt you. I'm not that sort of person."

"I don't care what kind of person you are. Just get out."

"Okay."

He opens the door, gets hit with the blast of the cold wind. Claude charges up the lawn, barking and growling and flashing his teeth. He slams the door shut and twists the doorknob lock as if Claude might burst right through.

He turns around. "You've got to call off your dog."

The old man hesitates, wags the gun again. "All right. Move aside."

The man comes carefully out from behind the armchair. Some faint noise from a side room makes him turn his head a notch. Paul's fast. He jumps forward, grabs hold of the barrel. Using it for leverage, he drives the man back across the room, tears the gun from his hands, and pushes him into the armchair where the old man sits and looks wide-eyed at the shotgun aimed at his face.

Paul hears it now, a sound almost disappearing under the sound of Claude barking outside the front door. A baby whimpering in the other room, only partly crying, as if the baby hasn't fully woken up.

He lifts his eyebrows. "What's going on? Who's that?"

"My granddaughter. I'm the babysitter tonight. The kids went to a movie. They'll be back soon."

The baby gets a little louder, but the sound is still muffled, coming and going.

"What do you need to do?"

"Let's leave her out of this. Please."

Paul stares at him. "You think I'd hurt a baby?"

"You've got that shotgun, son. Stop waving it around."

"Get her back to sleep. We don't need a crying baby here." He walks behind the man, following with the shotgun, but keeping it aimed down at the floor. A nightlight in the room casts a yellow glow on a rickety-looking old crib. The old man swoops the baby gently up, soothes her on his shoulder. Her whimpering grows louder.

"She needs a bottle," the old man says. "Go to the kitchen. Get a bottle out of the fridge. It's all made up. Do it if you don't want her screaming."

"Oh, Jesus. I wish I'd never knocked on your fucking door."

"I never asked you to. Watch your language. The baby."

"Yeah, yeah, okay. Sorry. I'm not around babies that much."

He goes into the kitchen, gets out the bottle, and brings it to the old man who is now sitting back in the armchair holding the baby. He gives the old man the bottle and stands back, keeping an eye on them but holding the barrel of the shotgun away, aimed down at the floor. He watches in a kind of amazement as the baby pulls at the bottle with greedy little lips. He'd had a girlfriend once who'd wanted a baby. Maybe he ought to go back and look her up. She wasn't too far from here. Nebraska. Maybe she'd be happy to see him. Wouldn't that be something, if she opened the door and smiled, happy to see him. She'd had little gaps between her front teeth. But they were pretty gaps; he was okay with them. He had a thing about teeth. That girl in the bar had had great teeth.

By degrees the baby settles. The old man gets up slowly and carefully and he lies her back down in the crib, and they go back into the living room.

"Sit back down in the chair," Paul says.

"Take the keys to the truck. They're on the ring there, right where you were heading."

"You must think I'm a bad person."

The old man shakes his head. "No. Sometimes people end up in a bad way without knowing how they got there. But they can turn it around."

"All I wanted was to get out of the cold. It was all because of a girl. I liked this girl."

"Take the keys and go, son."

"I don't go around hurting people. I wasn't raised that way."

8

"I believe you."

"I'll go now. I don't even want your damn truck. Just call that dog off."

Headlights come from the driveway, shine through the front curtains. He looks at the old man, who takes a fast breath. "It's my son and daughter-in-law, coming for the baby. Please don't do anything to them. I won't say anything."

He looks at the old man. "We already had this conversation. I'm not like that."

Now a knocking on the door, movement of the knob, someone pushing against the door. More knocking.

"Get the baby," Paul says.

"Please."

His hands shake on the shotgun. "Get the goddamn baby."

The man makes a frightened sound in his throat, but he goes in to get the baby. When he comes out with her, Paul says, "Wrap her up good. It's cold out there. Take the baby and clear out of here."

The old man turns at the door, baby cradled in the blanket against his shoulder. "Turn yourself in, son. I'll spin it the best way I can." He pauses. "I would have let you in if it hadn't been for the baby. My son wouldn't forgive me for letting in a stranger. I would have let you in. I want you to know that."

"I don't give a damn. Just go."

The old man opens the door part way, wedges past the snarling dog as his son from the front porch says, "What the hell, Dad?"

"Go to the car, Jim."

"Dad? What's going on?"

"Walk, Jim, walk. Claude, move your ass!"

Paul locks the door behind them. He sits in the armchair, holding the gun across his lap, more tired than he's ever felt in his life. But not cold. He'll just sit here in the warmth and wait. The old man probably *would* have let him in. *Salt of the earth.* He wishes now he'd told him he believed him. He should have at least given the old man that, after all the trouble he's caused. The funny thing is he kind of liked the old man. On a better night he'd have had a beer with him and sat on the couch watching television while the old man talked about missing his wife, and he'd talk about missing his parents, and maybe they'd remember some old iron-assed sergeants who'd helped them keep their heads on straight. Before long the lights—more than one car now—shine through the front window, the cop lights spinning in the driveway and the yard, casting an eerie strobe light through the house, checkering, pulsing across the walls, and he hears static from their cop radios. *Why is there always static? Who is there to call? How many does it take?* He moves to the window, pulls the curtain back, stands there in the frame, holding the shotgun but not aiming it, waiting for the next move. *Good country cops, salt of the earth!* He thinks about busting out the glass, but it seems sort of dramatic, like a scene in a bad movie. Maybe he could drop back out that back window and make it across a field. Sure, get across a field, find a country road, hitch a ride, maybe say, *Hey, I heard there was a party somewhere out here. You going there?*

SARGE AND HOLLINGS

HOLLINGS IS THE BEST man in training, the strongest, the fastest, the toughest, but Sarge still gives him a hard time. Maybe he gives him a hard time *because* Hollings is the best man, even better than Sarge himself, and Sarge can't stand knowing that, and knowing that Hollings knows it too. So he gives Hollings shit over small things—he doesn't like the way Hollings makes his bunk, he doesn't like the way Hollings ties his boots, he doesn't even like the way Hollings eats in the mess hall. It's all bullshit—Hollings's bunk is impeccable, his shoelace bow is a work of art, and he is the neatest eater among us. No food ever slops down his chin or slips out the side of his mouth, and you only see his teeth, which are glossy white and well-formed, when he is smiling between bites. It is, in fact, an honor and a pleasure to watch Hollings eat. On the other hand, watching some of the boys eat is disgusting, and watching Sarge himself eat is scary. He doesn't drool, he doesn't chew with his mouth open, but he stares down at his meat as if it's his prey, then slices like a murderer. When I watch Sarge eat, I think of those wildlife shows where the lion leaps on the gazelle's neck.

When Sarge gives him shit about his bunk, pointing out a nonexistent error and screaming in his face, "Do you see what I am talking about?" Hollings nods affably. "Yes, Sarge, I see now that the corner of my blanket is ill-shaped. If anything, you are being too kind in your critique."

Sarge would clobber Hollings at such moments—he would

clobber any of the rest of us—but Hollings is a fourth-degree blackbelt in karate, a jiujitsu expert, a college wrestling champion. As well as being the strongest, the fastest, the toughest, Hollings is also the smartest of us. He enlisted when he was one semester short of a degree in English literature with a minor in philosophy *and* a minor in microbiology. Sarge knows that compared to Hollings he is a chump, and he knows that Hollings knows it too. The rest of us don't mind that Hollings is the smartest. We love Hollings. We trust that he will look after us once we go over.

Hollings can answer just about any question we ask him. But the one question he can't answer is why he joined up. We are sitting in a field. It is the last night we will have off before we go over. It's warm, the moon is out, and fireflies spark in the night. We're all drinking, getting drunk, though Hollings is only sipping on a beer. He says drinking dulls his senses, dulls his mind.

"Hell, that's what's it *for*," Buddy says, "I *like* having my mind dulled out." We all laugh, even Hollings.

"I guess so," he says. "I just like thinking. I like seeing where my thoughts go, and if I drink, I can't follow my thoughts as well."

"Where do your thoughts go?" I ask. I would like to know. I would like to know where Hollings's thoughts go because I would like to think like Hollings thinks.

He laughs. "That's the second question I can't answer. I could *try* to answer it." He sips his beer. "No, I guess I don't *want* to answer it. Maybe the answer would be disappointing. It would be disappointing to you, and it would be disappointing to me. Maybe it would be best if I just stared out and looked thoughtful and let you imagine that I am thinking about something profound."

We laugh, but we're not letting him off the hook yet. "So why? Why the hell did you join up? Or why didn't you finish college and come in as an officer?"

"That's the *last* thing I would want to be. An officer. The very last."

"Why?"

"If I were an officer, I would have to order you into combat. I would have to ask you to risk your lives. I couldn't do it. If you wanted to charge a machine-gun nest, I would try to talk you out of it. There will always be another machine-gun nest, but there is only one you."

He leaves us thinking about that for a while, but we come back at him again. "So why? Why did you join up?'

He sighs. 'I could give you the usual reasons—patriotism, duty, my old man served, that sort of thing." He swallows. "I believe I will have another beer after all." He hands off an empty and we eagerly give him a fresh one. "Or I could say it was for adventure, for experience, to say that I was there. There may be some truth in all of that, but it misses something. To be honest, I bet none of you can really say either."

We fall silent. We watch the fireflies light up in the night and feel the warm breeze until finally Buddy says, "Hell, I know why. They were going to throw me in jail otherwise."

We all crack up. We offer reasons. Getting away from home, from a girl, from a bust-ass job. But it all sounds like bullshit in the night.

Hollings says, "Maybe the most truthful answer is that I don't know, or if I do know, it's not that I don't want to tell you but that I don't want to tell myself. Maybe I'm afraid of what I would say. Maybe I'm afraid that it would sound false, or maybe I'm afraid it would sound too true and it would frighten me, or maybe I would realize what an idiot I am to be sitting in a field with you dumbfucks, going to get our asses shot off for no good reason at all, or a reason we can't even name. Does that make sense?"

"Yeah," we say. "Hell yes. Sort of."

He swallows, stares into the night. "Does it?"

When we go over, Sarge isn't reckless, exactly, but he's committed to getting the job done. He favors foot patrol, old-school style, while the rest of us would rather go into towns on a Humvee or a tank, take a look around and get the hell out, or, better yet, call for a drone strike. That doesn't do shit, he says. You need to kick down doors, you need to look under the floorboards, beneath the beds, find the bomb-making material, shit like that.

We patrol into a town on foot and in a narrow street lined by stucco houses the enemy appears suddenly on a rooftop across the street from us. Hollings spots the ambush in the nick of time and signals us to safety in a cobbled street around a corner, while he himself rolls in the street like the gymnast he once was and flips up to hurl a grenade over the rooftop, a perfect throw as one summer he set a record in minor league baseball, Double A, seventeen strikeouts in a row.

So we are not unhappy when Sarge is wounded and flown away in a chopper because Hollings takes over. Lieutenant Adams is *technically* in charge, but for all intents and purposes, Hollings is our leader and the lieutenant knows it and lets Hollings call the shots. It's not like we neglect our duty but we're more careful about the way we enter towns. And we're careful with the people too. Only shoot if absolutely necessary, Hollings says. Only kill if absolutely necessary.

We go deeper into the country. We suffer in the heat. The sands blow. At night Hollings reads us passages from *War and Peace*. Even during the peace sections he reads in a dramatic way that holds us captivated, voice rising and falling in the perfect pitch he developed from his roles in community theater. When we have gotten sleepy and turned in, Hollings disappears into the desert. In the morning he reappears. From town to town we go, and no one fires upon us. It is as if Hollings has worked some magic in the night, cast a spell. Villagers wave. Children follow our Humvees. We toss them candy.

Sarge comes back and early one morning he leads us into a shit-fire battle, scrambling from street to street as the enemy fires from above. Buddy goes down and Hollings drags him into a doorway as

Sarge and the rest of us tattoo the rooftops with rifle fire until there is stillness except for the lingering resonance of gunfire that swells the head, fills the ears even after the shooting is over, but there is nothing that saves us from the sight of Buddy, blood spurting out of his throat, while Ransom, our medic, frantically bandages, and Hollings pumps at his chest to try to restart his heart and he keeps pumping long after it doesn't make sense to do so anymore.

Sarge touches his shoulder and I think maybe this is it, where they're finally going to have it out, but when Sarge says, "Let it go, he's gone," it's the quietest and softest I've ever heard Sarge's voice, and for a moment I think they might become friends. Hollings stops pumping and kneels over Buddy, murmuring some sort of prayer. It's hard to tell what prayers he's saying or even what faith he's calling upon, but he kneels over Buddy as if he's trying to send his spirit home, to its true home.

We're pulled back, set up in tents and sandbagged in and we have a good week of playing cards, drinking beer, and even Hollings has a few beers some nights. A new guy comes in to take Buddy's place. One night Sarge comes into the big tent where Hollings and some of the guys are resting on their cots. "We move out tomorrow," Sarge says. "We're going back in." He looks at equipment and weapons scattered about the tent. "This is a pigsty," he screams. "This is a shithole. You, new guy, pick this shit up!" The new guy, not much more than a kid, trembles a little. He tries to pick things up, but Sarge's screaming voice makes him awkward and he drops a box of ammo, which makes Sarge scream, "You trying to get us all blown to shit!"

Hollings is on his cot, staring up at the tent top, looking thoughtful like he had that night beneath the stars. "Lay off him. I'll clean it up."

"I didn't say you. I said him! You! New guy, move your ass!"

We're all looking at Hollings. We know we're going back into the shit tomorrow and no one should be yelled at, not tonight, not when it could be the last night, and we all know it's not really the kid he's yelling at.

Hollings slowly rolls on his side. "Leave the kid out of this."

A kind of shudder goes through Sarge's shoulders. He breathes out hard like a man who has been fighting something inside for a long time and is now giving himself up to that thing he has been fighting. "Okay, Hollings," he says, "Okay. It's time. You and me. How do you want to do it, bare hands or with gloves?"

Hollings sighs and rises from his cot. "Pistols at twenty paces."

Sarge is not one to stammer or to blink hard, but that is exactly what he does. He blinks hard and he stammers before he finds his words. "What do you mean pistols?'

"Pistols. A duel. Old-school. We march off twenty paces, turn, and fire."

Sarge's eyes flutter as he calculates. Sarge is a crack shot, and the one area where Hollings tested only average was in pistol shooting at close range. Only men on the verge of insanity would engage in this duel, but a cruel grin comes to Sarge's face. "You got it. See you outside in five minutes."

"Don't you want to wait for morning?" Hollings asks. "That would be more traditional. Pistols at dawn." And I get it, I think, and for a moment I think I might be thinking like Hollings thinks. Hollings has been joking, trying to point out the absurdity of the whole situation, the whole absurdity that has led us here, to this place and time, to this desert, and now he's trying to let Sarge in on the joke, get him to see this trap we're all in, the trap of life that gets everybody, here, back home, wherever it might be, the trap of time and place and the very nature of life and death and the way time kills us all, slowly, or all at once, and on a more practical level, he's simply giving Sarge a chance to cool down, to back off, giving them both a chance to back off and cool down. But Sarge's voice breaks with a high note of hysteria. "Why wait? Let's get it done."

Only men on the verge of insanity would not stop such a fight, and when Sarge heads for his own tent to get his gun, we urge

Hollings to stay put, to forget it, but in fact we are all a little insane after all and maybe we are secretly urging him on because we want him to kill Sarge for us because we're afraid Sarge will eventually get us all killed.

Still, we make an effort. One of the guys runs off to find the lieutenant and the rest of us take hold of Hollings physically, try to hold him down on the cot, though we know he could throw us all off if he wanted to. But he only chuckles and says, "Boys, let me go. I've got a plan here."

We let him go as he picks up his pistol from under his cot. He turns from us, checking it over. He turns back and says, "Don't worry. We'll just fire over each other's heads. Then we'll shake hands and we'll be done with it. That's how these things work. We'll hug and laugh about it."

They meet in the narrow corridor of sand between the tents on either side. They nod at one another with no expression on their faces, like two boxers meeting in the ring and touching gloves before a fight. The moon is full, the night bright, the hot air breathing over us. They stand back to back and walk off the paces, no one calling out, just each man counting quietly to himself, but they're being scrupulously fair about it because they both turn at the same time and raise their pistols. The sound is deafening in the night, despite all the gunshots we've heard, and it's as if the explosion keeps us from noticing for a moment that only one gun has fired, a moment before it registers that Hollings is falling backward, his body straight as a tree. You would think such a strong man would put up a fight for his life, that he would not be killed easily, but Hollings never moves at all, makes no sound as we try to hold in the blood pouring out of his chest and we cry for him to hold on, but none of it matters at all to Hollings. He only stares up at the stars, eyes wide and unblinking.

We surround Sarge, watch him as one might watch a mad dog, watch him as if we expect him to bolt into the desert. But we don't move in too close because he's still got the gun in his hand.

Lieutenant Adams runs out of the night, calling out desperately, "Stop! Stop!" as if he can turn back time. Sarge just stands there, without moving, his head hanging down, until I go over and take the gun out of his hand.

When the military police arrive to take Sarge away, they discover Hollings's gun was not even loaded.

Before they take us off one by one to get the full story, we stand in the moonlight with the lieutenant. He stares at us in a kind of horror. "Why would he do this? What was he thinking?" he asks of us, though it's really Hollings he's trying to ask. It's the last question Hollings can't answer, so I try to answer for him, but the lieutenant just stares at me as if he thinks that I, too, have gone crazy.

WHERE ARE YOU
GOING WITH HIM?

IT WAS A HOT afternoon in summer, a Sunday, and I was coming back from the market, headed to my apartment. I looked forward to having dinner alone at home and then going out to a bar on the town square. I felt little need to be with other people during the day, but by night I felt lonely and wanted company and conversations. I was sweating in the heat and I was eager to get back to my apartment, which stayed cool and dark if I kept the shutters closed.

On a cobblestone side street two men stumbled out of a cantina and began to swing awkward, looping, drunken punches at each other. I receded into a doorway, not really knowing what to do, if anything. From their clothes they appeared to be campesinos from the countryside. Sunday was their day to come into town to church and the market and there were some who resisted the evening call of home and lingered too long in the cantinas. One man wore a gray shirt and a straw sombrero that dangled on his back, held by a long string around his neck. One of his sandals was missing, and dried, caked blood coated his ankle. He was smaller than the other man and at first he was getting the worst of the fight. Their brawl had gained the attention of a handful of passersby, and a few people leaned out from windows overlooking the street, but the wild punches seemed so inefficient and harmless that the few observers were amused more than alarmed. In my life I have intervened a few times to stop fights, and other times I have ignobly walked away.

Since no one else seemed upset by the fight, I decided it wasn't really my place to do anything about it.

I was relieved when the men embraced like brothers and headed back into the cantina, but I'd only taken a few steps when they stumbled back out of the cantina and went at each other again. There was more intensity to the fight this time, and now the mood of the onlookers changed and they moved closer and urged the men to stop, and I also moved in closer from my doorway. The smaller, gray-shirted man was now a little quicker and his fists targeted in on the larger man's face and made him step back. The larger man stooped, picked up a rock, and struck the smaller man in the side of the head. The onlookers let out a kind of collective gasp, a sort of wordless, whooshing sound. Blood appeared on the face of the smaller man and dripped down the shoulders of his gray shirt. He almost fell, righted himself, and ran forward with all his force, shoving the other man in his chest. The large man fell backward and the back of his head slammed down on the cobblestones. There was again that terrible collective gasp and whooshing sound. The man lay perfectly still, and then blood, a halo of blood, ran out of the man's head and spread about him on the cobblestones.

The man with one sandal looked down at the fallen man, threw his arms in the air in a gesture of despair, and hobbled up the street, his shoeless foot dragging behind. He turned a corner and disappeared. We heard police whistles coming closer, and then four blue-shirted police arrived, panting, out of breath. Two crouched over the fallen man, saw that he was beyond help, and stood back up. Someone pointed and the two others ran up the street and turned the corner.

One thing I found curious, and still do, is that until that moment no one else had come out of the cantina, but now one man appeared in the doorway. The policemen looked up at him and the man disappeared inside. The police, nightsticks in hand, followed him into the cantina. At this point, the shutters of the windows closed and the few onlookers dispersed, and I dispersed with them.

It occurred to me that I could be asked to be a witness. I had a bad experience in my teens when I was arrested and I've been frightened of the police ever since, though there have certainly been times when I was reassured by their presence. At any rate, the last thing I wanted was to be caught up in this episode. I'd just finished college and had planned on staying in town for at least six months and hoped to do some good writing while I was here. I didn't want any complications.

After I ate supper I went to a bar on the square, one frequented by Americans and other foreigners. After a few drinks I usually felt talkative. I wanted to tell someone, anyone, about what I had witnessed, but again there was this fear of being drawn into the matter. If people knew that I'd witnessed a murder, or a killing, anyway, the word might spread and one day there would be a knock on my door and I would come down the stairs to find blue-shirted policemen standing there. They might ask me what I had seen. They might ask me why I had walked away from the scene of a crime.

I woke that night in a sweat. I do not need actual policemen at my door. The thought of policemen is enough. There are policemen at the door whether they are actually there or not. They are always at my door. Knocking at all hours. *My God, I might as well admit it now. I killed the man! I confess, I confess!* Cease, mind, desist! With such thoughts, I tumbled in and out of sleep.

I got up just after dawn and after a cup of instant Nescafé, double the recommended spoonful, loaded with cream and sugar, my mind cut me some slack and stopped attacking me. The policemen parted for a distant country. What would they really want with me, a young American? It was pretty obvious what had happened. Other people had seen it. They certainly didn't need *me* mucking up their investigation. This wasn't a matter of Porfiry sleuthing after Raskolnikov. Nobody gave a damn about what I had seen. But with that thought I felt sad. Here was a dead man, and a man on the run, and no one cared enough to track me down to ask me what

I'd seen. I felt sad for both men. Blood in the street and no one to give a damn.

I liked to walk in the countryside early in the morning. The high desert reminded me of New Mexico, where I had grown up. Though it was summer the mornings were still cool, and I wore a white wraparound Mexican sweater, huaraches, a sombrero, and to complete the effect, I carried a wineskin flask slung around my neck. I did not really mean to strike a pose, but I supposed if my attire attracted the interest of a young woman, I would have no objections. It wasn't that great a pose anyway. I usually only carried water in the wineskin. I didn't have a canteen so it was the easiest way of packing water.

To go into the countryside I usually first walked down a cobblestone street to a park. One could walk through the park or to the left there was a narrow road that skirted the park. At the juncture of the park and the road there was a space large enough for three or four cars. Before entering the park I checked on my own car, an old, blue Volkswagen. I hadn't intended to own a car, but someone leaving town suddenly had sold it to me for a few hundred dollars. It wasn't dependable enough for long trips, but it had come in handy for short excursions. When I'd first parked there a group of teens had told me they'd keep an eye on it for me for a few pesos each week and I got the gist of their meaning and paid up.

There was no one in the park at this hour. Normally I would cross some pleasant tree and flower-lined paths to the other side of the park and climb a dirt road for a mile and then come to a mesa. I could walk across the mesa for hours if I wanted, though usually an hour in each direction was enough for me. Then I'd go home and grab a small pack with my notebook and pen and I'd be off to a café to write. I liked to keep my days quite regimented.

In the park today, on the walking path, I turned a corner and came upon a man lying face down, apparently unconscious. He'd lost the sombrero somewhere along the way, but I recognized the gray shirt and the bare foot with the caked blood around the ankle.

The expression that one froze in place is, of course, a cliché. But indeed, I froze in place and looked down on the man. It would be hard to describe my thoughts because there was nothing in my mind that resembled a coherent thought. Now that I am almost seventy my wife tells me that I too often stare in a profound stupor until she waves her hand in front of my face. This staring worries her. But I'm not so sure it has to do with age. All my life, at a certain level of surprise, when I really don't know what to make of things, I stop and stare. I'd like to think that I am processing, but I don't know. I go blank.

The mental gears were just starting to move again with certain considerations. First off, I took note that we were alone, just the two of us, so whatever was decided in the next moments would be just between the two of us. Indeed, since he appeared unconscious, I supposed it was really only up to me what happened next. I could continue my walk into the countryside and certainly by the time I returned someone else would have found him and he would become *their* responsibility. That seemed like not a bad plan. A damn fine plan! That other person would do a much superior job, make better choices, so really I would be doing everyone a favor by walking on. But the hike was ruined. So maybe I should just turn around and go back to town and head to a café. I wondered, and I still wonder, what would I have done if I'd back in the States? Would I do something differently? As a foreigner was I more free or less free to act?

He was, obviously, a wanted man. I might go to the police. But that consideration didn't even make a half turn in my mind before it exited. If I could have choreographed myself to show my mental state, I might have shown a man walking in place, swinging his arms but going nowhere. I don't recall now but that might have been precisely what I did.

The mental gears moved a bit more and told me that this indecision would have to come to an end in some way, that I could not simply stay there walking in place for the remainder of the day.

The man himself set things into motion. He moaned and rolled on his side and opened his eyes, blinking, startled to find me standing above him. His face was streaked with dried blood. He had taken quite a beating in the fight. When I think of the man, when I think of the incident, I think of blood. The blood on his ankle, the blood on his face, the blood of the other man in the street, the way it ran out of his head in a gush. I've lived a quiet life, but I've too often found bodies covered with blood.

At any rate, this was a complication. There was no longer an unconscious man to simply walk past but an injured person who might need medical attention. He did not speak but raised a shaky hand and pointed at my wineskin flask. Not much choice here, really. I might have been able to feebly justify walking past him, but now I'd be a real jerk to deny him a drink.

I unslung the flask, opened it for him, squatted down, and he sat up and accepted it in both hands and raised it to his lips. His eyes widened, registered a note of surprise; disappointment perhaps. He moved the flask away from his mouth, looked at me, shrugged in resignation, and then raised the flask once more and drank deeply now, drank with a parched mouth and throat. He lowered the flask, breathed, drank long again, gave me a gentle, grateful smile.

My Spanish was limited and his Spanish was different from the kind one heard in town, so throughout our encounter, we accompanied our conversation with gestures. I indicated the side of his bloody head. "Necessita doctor?"

He shook his head vigorously. He stood, wobbled, and I took hold of his arm and steadied him. I asked him where he was going. He gestured in the direction of the mesa and muttered, "Mi familia."

I had been told that there was a village on the far side of the mesa, accessible by road. His family apparently lived in that village. It was several miles away, and he looked in no shape to walk there.

We were at another impasse. I'd given him a drink. I hadn't

called the police on him, had vaguely offered to summon a doctor. We were squared away, more than squared.

His eyes roamed the park. His body trembled. "Tengo miedo," he said. I am afraid.

He couldn't have seen or noticed me the day before, but I was convinced that he knew that I had seen the fight. It may have been that, in his guilt, he felt all eyes cast upon him.

"Policia?" Was he afraid of the police? I was searching for the words for self-defense, to tell him that there was an argument he could make there, that all was not lost.

He shrugged as if he wasn't much worried about that. He said, "Los hermanos." The brothers of the man. He drew his finger across his throat. Oddly enough, it did not strike me as melodramatic.

A few walkers were starting to show up in the park. Down one path vendors were setting up beneath the trees. He would be discovered soon.

"Mi familia," he said again. He took a few hobbling steps. It would take him hours. He'd be defenseless if the brothers came upon him. My voice shook, but I called to his back, "Tengo coche."

Now it was his turn to freeze in place. He stood with his back to me, undecided whether to go on or turn back. I wished him to go on. I'd made the gesture, that was enough, I was covered. He wouldn't haunt my dreams. Shit. His shoulders turned, then the rest of him. "Mi familia," he said. Yes, yes, the family, certainly the family. I sighed. There were tears in his eyes. I nodded. I would take him to his family. We went out of the park toward my car. He mostly walked on his own, but every few feet he leaned against me. At the edge of the park, before we came to the street, a man was coming toward us. I had noticed him in town before. I might even have said hello to him in the bar. He was a trim, middle-aged American with short hair and a stern face. It was difficult to place him neatly in the context of the town. Most foreigners here at least made some nod to fashion—wore sandals maybe, or a Mexican shirt, or maybe wore something artistic, a beret, or wore their hair long or in a ponytail, who knows—something that said, Hey, I'm not just a middle-class American. I'm a groovy sort of guy. But he wore dress slacks and a long-sleeved collared shirt, a man out of a JCPenney commercial. He always made me nervous when I saw him. He never smiled. He exuded disapproval. He was not a policeman, but his sort also frequently showed up and confronted me with skeptical looks. He had one of those faces where he could have been anything from ex-military to an accountant fleeing an embezzlement charge. He might make a discreet assassin. In fact, hadn't someone once whispered to me that he'd been a mercenary in South Africa, or was I conflating him with someone else, misremembering some late-night conversation?

He took in the sight of us, my new friend limping alongside me. His metallic eyes turned a notch flintier, shot out suspicious beams, not so much at my friend but at me. "Where are you going with him?" he asked. He shook his head in further disapproval but passed on without stopping.

In the years since, the line has lingered in my mind. Where are you going with him? Was it right for me to help him escape? Was it wrong? I had a priest friend once. We were workout buddies and when we were walking around a track together one day I tried to confess what had happened. He said it didn't sound like a sin to him, but since it bothered me, he said he would give me a general absolution for that and all the other things I probably wasn't telling him. I wasn't satisfied with the absolution, though, and a couple of weeks later I brought it up again. "But was it right?" I asked him over coffee at a café. He stared at his cup. "I can't say that for you," he said. "It seemed well-intentioned, anyway." He looked out the window, then back and said, "What would you have done in the States?"

The sun was full up now, a bright bead shining over the town. It was not hot yet, but I was sweating and the policemen were beating at my temples. I wished that the teenagers had damaged my car, stolen the tires, given me a reprieve. I turned back to the park to make sure the stern man wasn't watching us. I didn't see him, but I sensed him in the trees, taking note. But the wanted man and I were connected now in a strange alliance. I gestured for him to get in the car. Maybe it wouldn't start. But it did. The idiotic little car far outplayed its weight with an explosive bang. It rumbled, it roared, it announced our departure to the town. Hey, everybody, we're driving now!

I hadn't told him to do so, but as in gangster movies, he slumped way down against the door, concealing himself except to see over the dashboard enough to give directions. We went up the road that ran to the side of the park. Only once a car came from the other direction and he sank deeper as it passed. We merged with a wider road, and with a pang of regret I looked to my right at the peaceful mesa where I might have been walking this very morning with my cheery little wineskin.

After five miles or so he signaled abruptly, forcefully, for me to slow. There was a tiny wooden sign with an arrow and the name of a town with an Indian-sounding name. We turned and we were on a bumpy dirt road now, increasingly pitted as we drove on. The little Bug shuddered, shook my spine. My hands vibrated on the steering wheel as we bellied over potholes and forded muddy creek bottoms. We wound around the mesa, climbed a switchback road, and we were into a lightly forested area of juniper and sage, and there were small branch-offs, not exactly roads but paths, and through the trees I glimpsed a few small, squat adobe homes, spread out through the forest. There was no main hub to the village as far as I could tell; just this scattering of small homes in the trees.

My friend had grown increasingly agitated as if he sensed the brothers might appear at any minute. His eyes scanned about. He signaled me to stop. To the left, maybe twenty yards down a dirt path, I saw a woman and two children, a boy and a girl, around six or seven, come out the front door. They stood in a small cactus-studded yard with a clothesline in front. A white sheet hung down from the line. The woman gathered the children close and they partially hid behind the hanging sheet and stared at the car. Well, this was it then. I'd drop the man, turn about, and go. Case closed. He'd have to deal with the brothers himself.

Urgently, though, he signaled me to wait. He smiled, kept making the wait gesture, his smile eager and gracious as if he had some gift he wanted to give me for my help. As he got out of the car, the wife and children hurried toward him. There was just enough room to swing the tiny car out to the right and then back to the left to complete a U-turn so that I could hustle the hell out of there. I'm not sure, really, if I would have stopped and waited or not, but there wasn't a choice now, as he'd come back into the road and stood blocking my way, holding his hands up like a traffic cop. He wagged a finger at me again to wait, a sort of friendly, admonishing gesture, then he joined his wife and children and they went back into the house. Before, I could have pretended to myself that driving off without further notice was fine, but this added move of stepping into the road to block my path made the driving off now seem actively cold.

I waited. I looked in the mirror, to the sides, watching for the brothers. I'd only give this another minute, two at the most. My hand was already on the stick shift, ready to go into gear, when they came out of the house into the sunlight, each carrying a small bundle. Oh my God. But events were already in motion. The woman and the two children climbed into the back with their bundles and the man resumed his place in front. He shrugged apologetically. He'd at least had time to wipe the blood from his face and he now wore two old tennis shoes.

As we were going down the dirt road, a battered gray pickup was coming from the opposite direction. The man spoke to his wife and children and now they all went into a fugitive duck.

Three broad-shoulder men—or at least they appeared broad-shouldered since they were side by side—three abreast in the front seat of the pickup, came alongside us. I felt their eyes on me. I waved in as nonchalant a way as possible, while at the same time trying not to appear overly nonchalant, which would be a tipoff, and we were fortunate in that the narrowness of the road made them veer into the grass and dip down and my car to tilt up so that they had no clear view of the interior of my car as we passed each other.

I glanced over. "Los hermanos?"

He nodded. "Los hermanos."

I waited a half minute before looking back in the mirror. I saw a shiny glint, and I could not tell whether the truck was going on or turning about. I gunned the little spitfire of a car, gassed the hell out of it, beat the underside to shit as we barreled over the potholes and muddy creek beds, and the woman made a sound in her throat. The man looked back and groaned and the children leaned into one another.

If they followed, they might have thought we turned back toward the town. But the man directed me in the other direction, to a larger city with a large bus station. On the forty-minute drive I looked in the mirror over and over.

I found a place to park at the station, and we stood at the car to say goodbye. Maybe they were going to the border. I don't know. I thought he said something about a brother of his own who lived elsewhere. The children looked quiet and sad, huddled against their mother, her arms around them. The woman looked resolute, heading into whatever new life awaited them, whatever life was like for people setting forth with few possessions in their hands. If they would be okay, I thought, it would be because of her. I tried to give them what I had in my wallet, the equivalent of thirty bucks or so, but they wouldn't take it. The man shook my hand, a soft, gentle touch. The woman gave me a sweet, timid smile, an unfathomable smile, really. She looked not much older than I was. The children stared at me with large eyes as they leaned against her legs. Then they all went into the station. My shirt was soaked with sweat, but I was relieved to be done with them.

A week later I was walking toward the town square when the

grim American came walking from the other direction. I prepared myself to ward off any questions or accusations that might come my way. But he did not look toward me, did not acknowledge me. His stony stare into the distance made too much a point of not acknowledging me.

Some weeks ago, these many years later, I was at a conference, staying at a hotel with an atrium and many high floors above. I had just come out of a small hotel office space for guests, where I had printed some pages. A woman fell screaming from the top floor and landed in the atrium only a few feet away from me with a sickening thump. The blood gushed out of her head, formed a kind of halo around her head. A few of us looked at her and each other in horror. She had white hair, appeared about my own age, and looked relatively undamaged except for the pool of blood. Her eyes were open and looked like dull chips of plastic.

I bent over her for a second, gagged, thought briefly of staunching the blood with my sweater, but another person at the conference, a nurse by profession, said that she was dead. I went and sat down at a table, out of the line of view of the body. I looked at my hands. They were shaking. I noticed some flecks of blood on my pages. It took surprisingly long for a few policemen to arrive, and then for an ambulance to show up and take her away. Throughout all this time, there was surprisingly little fuss in the hotel. Large potted trees and plants surrounded the area where she had fallen, obscuring the view. On the far side of the atrium the meal service was still going on at the restaurant and at the front desk people were still checking in and out. Business went on as usual, as if people were always falling to their deaths at the hotel. Nothing to see here.

The two deaths merge in my mind, perhaps because of the image, the way the blood ran out, formed pools around their heads.

My priest friend has drifted from my life now, but I think of his question on occasion and the circumstances that make us intervene sometimes and not at other times, and I wish there had been an earlier intervention. We did not know the way that it would end, but what I am really wishing is that I—all of us—had done more in that street to stop the fight. I wish there had been someone on the top floor to hold the woman back from jumping.

The days disappear rapidly now. I don't like complications, but in the night people show up. The policemen, the dead man in the street, the falling woman, the disapproving American, the fleeing family. Others too, of course, a whole lifetime of people: my parents, my siblings, my children, my wife, friends, neighbors, strangers, as if we are all gathering together to make one last great escape.

CONVERGENCE

I MISS MY DAYS at Lou Bonavento's Boxing Gym, even though I was never a very good boxer. I was too polite for a boxer, too concerned about the welfare of my sparring partners. After I was chased around the ring one afternoon, Lou draped a heavy arm over my shoulders. "Look, Danny," he said. "I like that you're a nice guy and all, but what would make you mad enough to really fight?"

I thought about it, said finally, "I guess if anybody messed with my wife or kid."

"Good," he said. "Visualize that. Some freako punk after them."

Still, it was sweet after boxing, stepping into a crisp autumn afternoon, sailing forth from the gym with a cracked lip, bruised ribs. It made me happy to go home, to have Jenny bandage my wounds, to fuss over me, to tell me I was stupid for boxing.

I didn't tell Lou when Jenny got sick. I just drifted off. I didn't return his calls. I feel badly about that. He was a good guy and I hurt his feelings.

I went out to dinner with some friends last night, a couple Jenny and I used to get together with. It was a pleasant September evening, cool with a hint of coming fall, but I just kept thinking about getting home to Matt. We were at an outdoor café in a suburban neighborhood, and I told my friends about Matt's new middle school, where some of the kids seem old and jaded beyond their years. They slouch against the lockers, in leather jackets and chains. With hooded eyes they watch the hallways for prey.

After I'd filled them in on Matt, I didn't have much to say. I drank coffee and stared out at a sky turning dark with clouds. They pitched into a description of their lives with their kids, toddlers still, and I found I didn't care much about what their kids ate or how much they slept or what cute thing they'd said, though I remembered talking excitedly about all that sort of stuff when Matt was little.

They stopped talking and Barb reached across the table, squeezed my hand, and asked, "How are you, really?" As she stared soulfully into my eyes, I wanted to hurtle the low white picket fence that encased the café patio. I'd race for my car and escape.

"It has been nice to see you," I said. "This has been really nice."

The boxing gym is still there. I drive by it now and then, not intentionally, but my sales calls take me past it. It's a squat, flat, gray building behind a car wash and across the street from a blood bank. One window has been boarded up for as long as I remember. On rainy days Lou would stick buckets out to catch the water leaking through the roof, and the gym always had a moldy smell. Sometimes I consider boxing again, but it wouldn't be much fun without Jenny there to tend my wounds, to cluck and brood over me and tell me I'm too old for this sort of stuff. I think about just stopping by to say hello to Lou, but then I'd have to explain what happened to Jenny, and if I don't talk about it, if I don't tell anybody, it's almost like for a day or two, an hour now and then, I can pretend she isn't gone.

As I'm driving in my car my cell phone rings and my ears blur and I go into a sort of panic as I hear something about the school and Matt being sick, and then the words start coming in more clearly. "Mr. Thompson, this is Sally, the school nurse. Everything's fine, don't be alarmed. Matt is just sick to his stomach. I've got him in the health room if you want to come by and check on him."

In the health room Matt lies on an examination table, hands over his belly, staring up the ceiling. He looks pale, but he smiles wanly when he sees me. "Hi, Dad. I'm okay."

Sally is short and slender, with curly dark hair, and as she deals with another kid sitting in a chair, she calls out in a cheery, battle-hearty voice, "I'll be right with you, Mr. Thompson. We've got a bee-sting kid here."

The bee-sting kid says, "I feel the pain all the way up to here." He indicates his neck. His scraggly dark locks fall into his eyes. "It got me on the hand, but it hurts way up past my arm, all the way up here to my neck."

"Can you breathe okay?" Sally asks.

He takes a couple of breaths. "When I breathe in it feels pretty good," he says, "but when I breathe out it feels kind of stuck."

"Do you know if you're allergic to bee stings?" Sally asks.

"I don't know. I got bit before, but I think it was yellowjackets."

"So you don't know if you're allergic to bees?"

"I don't know. But I had an uncle who died of a sting."

"Breathe, Andrew. Your mother will be here in a minute. "

Andrew shrugs. "Whatever." He looks over at Matt, who's still lying on the table. "They'll kill you with the food here. Bring your own lunch."

Sally turns back to me and looks at me with friendly brown eyes. "It's your call," she says. "He doesn't have a fever or any other symptoms. You can take him home or wait and see if he feels better. We see a lot of this with the new middle schoolers. It's an adjustment being in with the older kids. Nerves."

I'm ready to take him home, but Matt sits up and says he wants to finish the afternoon at school.

The next day Sally calls me again on my cell phone. She gives a sympathetic chuckle. "Well, Mr. Thompson, I'm sure you don't want to hear this, but Matt threw up again today."

When I go in today, Matt's got that same pale look he had the day before, and his lip trembles a little. "Hey, Dad," he says. "I'm okay."

I pat him on the shoulder. "I can take you home." I look at Sally. "How's the bee-sting kid?"

Sally laughs. "Andrew was fine. His mother said she didn't know anything about an uncle who died."

A couple of days later she calls again, and this time her voice sounds concerned and I drive quickly, my heart racing as she comes out of the health room and meets me in the hallway. "Dan," she says, and I like the way she uses my first name this time. "I think something's going on here."

"Nerves?"

She frowns. "I think something's causing the nerves."

My throat tightens up. I'm going to get a lecture that I'm doing something wrong, but she reaches out and touches me on the shoulder, actually sort of pats me like you might a child. "I think one of the bigger kids is bullying him. He wouldn't say so, but I suspect."

She looks into my eyes and she sees something there that makes her own eyes widen in alarm. "It will be okay, Dan. If something's going on, we'll stop it."

I realize I've made a fist and I'm punching it into my palm. She squeezes the fist, to hold it in place. "I'll keep tabs on him. Let's see if he's well enough to stay."

We go into the health room, and I stand over the examination table, looking down at his wan face. If it is some kid bullying him, I can't even punch him out. If it were only somebody older, a crazy teacher or coach, I could do something. Meanwhile Sally has been called into action. Andrew's back. He's gotten it on the lip this time, right on the playground as he was sipping on a can of juice. His bottom lip puffs out. "Bees suck," he says.

I nod. "Sorry, Andrew. Watch out for them." I squeeze Matt's shoulder. "What's going on, champ?"

He shrugs. "Nothing. My stomach just feels weird."

"Is somebody bothering you?"

"I don't want to talk about it, Dad."

It's not unusual that I'm giving Matt a boxing lesson this weekend. I've given him plenty of boxing lessons over the years. So it's not like I'm giving him the *Listen, kid, this is the way we men deal with things* pep talk. That's not it at all. We just happen to pass in the hallway Sunday evening and we kind of start play boxing like we've done a hundred times before. I sort of juke around in the hallway so he can't step past me. He grins, gets into it with me. "Guard your head," I remind him when he throws a jab. "Don't drop your hands. Always guard your head."

"Hey, Ali dropped his hands all the time," he says.

It's the argument he always gives me, drawing from the boxing footage we've watched together, and I give him back my usual. "Ali could do whatever he wanted because he *was* Ali . . . Guard your head. Jab, jab, jab, right cross, left hook, faster, throw it faster. Guard your head. Always guard your head."

As we juke around in the hallway, my breath quickening, into my mind pops this lesson my father gave me once. It's one of those memories that float in out of nowhere, through a haze of years. I'm a kid, in my old bedroom, and my father is trying to teach me how to properly fold and hang up my trousers. Each time I try to do it I somehow get the crease messed up. It's never right. The trousers look okay on the hanger to me, but he keeps saying they look sloppy. He shows me a pair of trousers that he has hung up. "They look the same to me," I say. "No, no, they don't look the same at all," he says, his voice getting tighter and louder. "This is the one *I* hung up; this is the one *you* hung up. Don't you see the difference—*don't you see it?*" But I don't. I don't see the difference. He's shaking the trousers in my face, the cloth scratching against my cheeks. He's yelling, "*Are you blind?*" and what I hear in my mind now, in his withering voice, is not only anger but fear. If he fails to teach me this essential lesson, I am doomed.

"Guard your head. See how I can slip this punch in if I want?"

"Dad," Matt says, clenching his teeth and ducking his head. "Is this supposed to be fun?"

On Monday morning he doesn't talk much on the drive to school. I point out the blue sky, the mountains in the distance, the sharpness in the air this morning as autumn sets in, but he only nods, mumbles, "Nice." I stop my car in the drop-off line in front of the school. He won't hug me goodbye here, not here where he might be seen.

He's said nothing about the bully, if there is one. Maybe there is no bully. But no, there's always a bully, and one only hopes, ignobly, that the bully moves on to other prey.

"Bye, Dad."

He's out the door and I watch as he merges with a throng of other kids approaching the front doors. A kid bangs into him and Matt stumbles sideways. I take a breath, but he rights himself. The other kid rushes on. Just an accident. Just a bunch of kids with overloaded backpacks converging on a crowded doorway.

The car behind me honks.

I go about my day, my cell phone on in case Sally calls. After lunch I'm starting to feel safer. I'm starting to think we're going to get through the day. But part of me wants to go into the health room. I want to check on old Andrew, to see where the bees have gotten him this time. Mostly, though, I feel a little something tingling around inside, a feeling sort of familiar, yet sort of surprising, and I realize I want to feel Sally's touch on my arm again, to have her look into my eyes and say my name.

I drive by the boxing gym, catch its flat, gray color out the corner of my eye. I start to go past as usual, but then I whip into the blood bank parking lot and swing the car around, cutting back across the street.

Instead of Lou a younger guy in boxing shorts and a T-shirt breaks off from the ring where he's giving instruction to two guys who are about to start sparring. He puts them on hold and slips through the ropes and approaches me with a salesman's bounce in his steps. "Can I help you?"

"Hi," I say, shaking his taped hand. He's got the sculpted body of a middleweight, the soft shake of a boxer. "I used to box here," I tell him. "I'm looking for Lou."

"I'm Ron. Lou sold the place to me six months ago." As he gives me a friendly grin, I see a flicker of silver in his mouth, a pierced tongue. I don't mind, but it's way different from Lou's style. He shrugs. "I kept the name for now because people know it."

"Oh." I stare out at the guys in the ring and try to take in the whole gym, the side canvasses, the heavy bags hanging from metal chains, a guy in the corner working the speed bag, someone jumping rope way back in the shadows.

"Well, if you see Lou, tell him Danny stopped by."

"Sure, man. Listen, you ought to come back. I've got all sorts of classes. I got something for everybody. Men, women, kids, seniors. Boxing's great conditioning for guys your age."

"Hey, do I look that old?" I step back from Ron. I go into a shadow boxing routine, throw a few jabs in the air, follow them up with a right cross and a left hook.

"Not bad," Ron says. "Not too bad, man."

I glide across the floor and slam my fist into a heavy bag. I wince and step back and try to wring the pain out of my wrist.

Ron looks alarmed, worried about liability issues. "You okay, man? You shouldn't do that without gloves."

I laugh. "I'm fine, man. Don't you know, I was the 174-pound, light-heavy, Rocky Mountain division B, second-class semichamp?" I narrow my eyes and say in my best Clint Eastwood, husky voice, "I was a legend."

He stares at me, taken aback for a moment before he laughs, the silver stud flicking on his tongue. The timer blares and he heads back to the ring, turning around to call, "Come back, man. Work out with us."

I look around, blinking. There are still buckets on the floor. Same leaky roof, same moldy smell. I smile at him, open my hands, palms up. *Who knows?*

HOLDOUTS

IN THE MIDDLE OF the night, getting out of bed to use the toilet, Ed has another fall, a real doozy this time. He smacks his head on the dresser, slides to the ground. Stuck on his back, the floor whirls beneath him until he's riding in a jeep with Dickey and Mart, winding along a dirt road, jungle on both sides, sweaty fatigues glued to his back. Mart's driving, a big, cheerful guy, a little older than Dickey and Ed, who are just a couple of years out of high school. The war's been over for six months and they're not expecting any trouble. They're not even armed, except for the pistol that Mart, an officer, carries in his holster. Mart outranks them, but they're all friends. Dickey and Ed are just supply clerks, arrived a few months earlier, never seen any action. When bullets tear into the jeep, Ed's first impression is that Mart's shirt is ripping around the chest. Mart makes a choking sound in his throat and the jeep plunges off the road and rolls down a hill into a ravine, the descent slowed by thick foliage. Ed bangs forward and back, sits stunned for a moment, with Mart slumped over the steering wheel. Bullets zing through the trees, dropping leaves on their heads, a rain of leaves. Dickey's crumpled up in the back and he thinks Dickey's been shot too, but Dickey stirs, raises his head. "Roll out," Ed says.

Ed drags Mart from the jeep and they take cover behind it. He cups his hands to Mart's chest, but blood flows through his fingers.

"Mart, Mart, it's going to be okay," Dickey says, as if he believes it somehow, as if he's talking to a kid who's fallen off a swing or something.

Mart's eyes are open but unseeing, and he's going into the shakes. Dickey holds his hand and keeps saying that he's going to be okay as Ed presses on his chest, trying to hold in the blood. There's a terrible blue-white color in Mart's face, and after a few seconds, the shaking stops. Ed puts his ear to Mart's mouth. Some sort of sound, maybe, in his throat, a kind of groan or escape of wind, but not a sound like breathing.

Dickey's shell-shocked. His face is pale, his lips trembling. He's small and thin, and he looks about fifteen years old, like one of the guys from Ed's football team. Ed knows he and Mart were close. Best friends.

Ed lifts the pistol from Mart's holster. He did pretty good with the gun training in basic, and he used to go hunting with his father. He wipes his hands through the grass, trying to clear them of Mart's blood. He braces his arms on the jeep hood and fires a couple of times across the road, figuring to back them up. Instead, they target in closer, bullets chopping at the metal of the jeep, zinging through the high grass.

"We've got to get out of here, Dickey. Retreat."

"What about Mart?"

"We can't help Mart now."

They run through the jungle, Ed breaking brush, panting, coaxing Dickey along. In a small clearing they pause. They're bent over, winded. Ed straightens to look around. He doesn't see or hear anyone coming. The jungle presses in around them, birds calling out in the trees.

Dickey's sniffling. "What if he's not dead?"

"He's dead, Dickey. He's dead."

Dickey looks back in the direction of the jeep, his shoulders heaving. "He ran off the road to save us. He saved us, Ed."

Ed nods. He doesn't really think Mart had a whole lot in mind with his chest all torn open. "He sure did. Now we have to save ourselves."

Invisible through the trees and brush, but not sounding far away, a man calls out and another man calls back. They were supposed to have surrendered! Maybe they don't even know the goddamn war is over.

"Come on, Dickey! We've got to run for it."

Okay, need to get off this damn floor. Roll. From back to stomach. Sure, no good on the back. Try the stomach. Then I can crawl, he thinks.

Dad? He can already hear that kind of tremulous sound in George's voice if he finds him down here. *Dad, we can't keep going this way. We need to give that assistant living place some more thought.*

Sure. Let's give it some more thought.

But it's too damn expensive. If he lets them lock him up, he won't have anything left to leave to the kids and grandkids. He can just as well die at home, and when he does the cleaning lady can find him and call someone.

But I really need to get to the toilet, he thinks, or I'm going to whiz all over myself and then the cleaning lady will tell the kids all about it. Where's a dog when you need one? There's always those movies where the dog comes in and saves you. I like dogs, but I wouldn't count on one to save me. Old Tex wouldn't have known what the hell to do. That's highly overrated, those saving dogs. It doesn't happen that frequently. I like a small dog. I like a dog to sit on my lap. I don't need one saving me all the time.

What the hell am I thinking here? I need to get to the toilet.

"C'mon, Dickey. Keep moving."

They've struck a grassy footpath, not quite a trail. To the right there's thick canopy, a mesh of fronds, broad wet leaves twisting in every direction. They chop with their hands to clear branches, fording into the jungle. He hears shouts, men on the hunt, but it's hard to tell where the voices are coming from; to the left, to the right, behind. He pulls Dickey down and they lie flat, below the vast leaves, the jungle unsettled by their presence, a kind of quivering and humming in the bush as if an alert has been sounded. They worm back, inches at a time, receding deeper into the jungle. The shouting moves farther away, and then disappears.

They've crawled back into some sort of muddy dip in the ground. A gassy, humid odor, not too unlike the bayous of Houston, rises in his nostrils. He takes comfort in the familiarity of the scent, notices the play of late afternoon light through the brush. The jungle isn't silent, speaks with a raucous symphony of birds and a sound like rushing water through the trees. Things don't seem so dangerous now. He's reminded of a game somehow, some kind of hide-and-seek game, which isn't right, he knows, to think of a game when Mart is dead. Maybe it only lasts a minute, maybe a couple of minutes. This sense of playing a game that comes over him, that blends in time with days adventuring near the bayous, dangerous with the gators if you didn't know what you were doing. But not dangerous like this. Not with men hunting him while he's thrilled with a delicious sense of invisibility. The jungle hums, as if it's humming for him alone because he knows Dickey is hearing something different. He will have to get up soon. He knows this. He will have to come out of the jungle and find his way back to base, and there will be his service to finish up, and he'll have to go home and do whatever it is a guy is supposed to do for the next fifty years of his life or however long he lives—the whole thing, marriage and kids and a car in the garage and a lawn to mow. As he lies there, savoring the sense of invisibility, he wonders if there might be something different for him, some place like Paris or New York City. Maybe he'll even go to an opera or something. Imagine that: him, Ed, at an opera. All that singing and dancing. He has a faint image of red velvet stairways and women in white blossoming dresses, the image probably from some movie he's seen. Who knows where he might go or what he might do with his life, but he wants just a little more time to ponder the possibilities. He never tells anybody about that feeling of wonder that came over him, even Lois. Maybe he hints at it some, but it's not right, enjoying himself, not with Mart dead. And it's probably weird anyway, all those thoughts.

He thinks of what will happen if they are found. No game. Maybe they should break for it now; head back to the road. Where the hell is the road? Good thing they don't move because the shouts of the holdouts, the calls to each other, come closer again. Dickey's back humps up as if he's about to rise and run, and Ed pushes his head down. He tilts his chin an inch, and through a gap in the low brush the boots of a soldier appear a few feet away. The boots stand in place as if that's all that exists of the soldier. The boots are splattered and old and battered, falling apart. The laces are missing from one boot and the other is held together by loops of old twine. One step closer and he'll fire, aiming straight up from between the rotting boots, right where the middle of the man will be, and at close range the .45 will do terrible damage. He supposes he should hate the man for killing Mart, for the horrible things that have happened in the war. But he hasn't been here long enough to hate anybody, has mostly only seen a few slumped, defeated Japanese prisoners. But if the man takes another step forward, he will fire and blow his chest apart.

The next thought that comes to him is of his mother hugging him before he leaves for basic, when the war was still on. "You don't need to be a hero. Just come home."

He hears voices, footsteps, other soldiers coming to join this one. Sweat rolls down Ed's forehead. *I'm not dying here!* He'll fire at the first one and take off running, and if Dickey can't keep up, he'll leave him behind.

The boot with the missing laces lifts and moves behind the other boot, toe touching the grass. The man says something to his friends, his voice high, nervous—young—shocking in the closeness of the sound. He pivots and the soldiers trot off.

"Come on, Dickey," Ed whispers in the bedroom. "I've got to take a leak real bad!" He crawls along the carpet, guided by the night-light in the bathroom. He pushes with his toes and knees, wedging and working his elbows against the carpet until the surface changes. Then he's on the cool tile of the bathroom. He crawls until he can get his hands on the sides of the toilet. Tucks his knees up. He pulls up on the edge of the toilet, tightens his stomach muscles—the core—they're always talking about moving from the core, whatever the hell that means. Straining his hands, arms, legs, back, stomach, the core, the damn core, he just makes it! Got it! He kneels over the toilet. But there's another setback. He draws in a strong odor of bleach—almost knocks him out. The cleaning lady overdoes it every time. She means well, makes him a nice sandwich when she's there, but she knocks the crap out of him with the bleach. He shakes his head to clear it. He holds the pajama waistband and the undies down, lets loose over the edge, some of it spraying and bucking back toward him, but he's going. Oh, yeah, that's good, that's good. He goes, pauses, goes, pauses, goes, come on now, come on, get it out. Oh, yeah. Ah, that's good. That's good. Relieved, he lies down on the cool tile, comfy now, comfy enough, a whole lot better than before. Rest up a little and make it back to bed.

As twilight settles in the bugs and mosquitoes are moving in on them in this squalid, fetid little mud hole. They're sitting up, and Ed is hearing something, some faint rumbling in the distance that might forebode something good. But now the sound fades off, and he thinks maybe he imagined it.

"You think we're lost, Ed?"

"We're okay. We've got a good hiding place."

"You're my best friend, Ed, you know that? Mart was my best friend. But now . . ."

"Thanks, Dickey. You're my best friend too." He supposes it's true enough for now, but it makes him feel bad for almost leaving Dickey behind. He hears that promising sound again. He listens, puts his finger to his lips.

Dickey's eyes widen. "You hear them? Are they coming back?"

"I think I hear a truck. Come on!"

They see the lights of two jeeps and a truck where their own jeep had swerved off the road. Men with guns, real soldiers, fighting men, fan out through the high grass.

Ed shouts to them, to let them know they're coming in, so they won't shoot. He pulls Dickey along by the arm. There's the jeep in the ravine, and in the moonlight they're carrying Mart, struggling with his weight. He blocks Dickey's view with his body.

"What happened?" a sergeant asks.

"Holdouts, I guess."

The sergeant shakes his head. "Hell of a thing at this stage in the game."

Crawling back toward the bed—so close now, if he can only get enough strength to climb back into it—he remembers the night Dickey came to dinner. A salesman, passing through Houston. It's 1960. They haven't seen each other since the war. Fifteen years. Dickey doesn't look much older, still short—of course he's still short—still thin. His hair's a little longer, slicked back. Ed's told the kids they need to be on their best behavior. He remembers that night at dinner, with Lois and George and Sis and Frank. They'd been polite kids that night, and Lois had been sweet to his old friend. Dickey's quiet, smiling a little, looking at the kids as if he's thinking about what good kids they are. They sit on the patio in the backyard. It's just a small backyard, a small ranch house, though a few years down the road there will be a bigger backyard and a bigger house, but Dickey thinks it's a nice place. He lives in an apartment in Chicago. Hard to get much of a word out of him, but he's pleased to be sitting on the patio and he says he likes the fireflies, the little sparks in the night.

Dickey tells them he's not married, but Lois says, "Oh, well, there must be a girl you're seeing? Someone special?" She gives him one of her great warm smiles. "She'd be lucky."

"No, not really. Nobody special." Dickey sits there with his own smile, not like Lois's, but nice in its own way: quiet, soft. He's looking at Lois and the kids, who are getting squirmy. Better ship them off to bed before they break down and show their true stripes.

Later they smoke cigarettes alone on the patio. They've each got a little glass of whiskey, though neither of them is a big drinker. Maybe it's just the thought of the whiskey, the taste it leaves, that loosens them up.

Dickey stares into the night, the fireflies sparking back by the alley. "I think about Mart sometimes."

"Yeah, I do too," Ed says, though this isn't really true. He hasn't thought much about either Mart or Dickey for years until Dickey called to say he was passing through.

"It shouldn't have happened that way."

"No, it shouldn't have happened."

"The war was over, Ed. That's what gets me. The war was over."

"Yeah, it was supposed to be."

"Mart must have been one of the last. One of the last to die. Imagine that. Imagine all the things in life Mart never had a chance to do."

They sit there, sipping so slowly it's almost as if they're only pretending to drink.

"I didn't want to leave him, Ed."

"I know."

"I keep thinking he wasn't dead, and we left him there."

Ed shuts his eyes. "Jesus, Dickey. I don't want to go into all this now."

"I don't blame you. You saved my life."

Ed feels something move inside his chest. "Knock it off. We saved ourselves."

"You're a lucky man," Dickey says, and it makes Ed feel like hell.

Lois has asked Dickey to stay over, but he says he needs to get on the road. Later, in bed, Lois says, "Did it all go okay? Did Dickey enjoy himself?"

Ed moves to the window and stares at the empty driveway, at the street and the corner lamp, the yellow glow of the light beneath. "Sure," he says. "It was good. He liked you and the kids."

Maybe Dickey will change his mind, turn around, spend the night with them. He wishes he could call Dickey back, feels a sudden pang of loss, even though he's just seen him. But if Dickey did turn around, what more was there to say? People had gone through a lot worse. It hadn't been much of a war for them.

"I like him too." She pauses. He can tell she's got more on her mind. "He didn't say much about himself."

"Dickey was always shy. He was never very confident."

She watches him as he undresses, turns off the light, climbs into bed. They lie side by side, breathing in the darkness. Over the years he's told her the rough outlines of that day, but only the rough outlines. The images of Mart's torn chest roll through his mind, the jeep plunging into the brush. Mart's blood slips through his fingers. He wipes his bloody hands through the grass. A sigh, a groan, in Mart's throat, but not breath, not really breath.

"Do you think he'll come back?"

"I don't know."

He rolls over on his side, and she follows, presses her body against his, her hand on his shoulder. Her voice is soft but insistent. "Did you talk about what happened?"

He's glad for the darkness of the room. "Sure, we talked."

In the morning the front door opens and George calls from the hallway. Damn, he's still on the carpet. He'd fallen asleep before he made it back to bed. George will insist he move in with him. Or this will give George more ammo to put him away in assisted living.

"*Dad?*"

Sure enough, there's George's leaning through the door, the face of an old guy. He still has trouble believing the white hair and moustache, as if George might be wearing some sort of disguise.

George has aged too fast. Never got married. Maybe if he'd gotten married, he would have taken better care of himself.

"Dad, are you okay?"

Ed gives a wave. "Just doing my push-ups. I'm trying to build back up."

"Jesus, Dad. You're wet."

"I got most of it in the toilet. Help me up. Let's get some breakfast."

George stoops, digs his fingers into his armpits, grunts, and struggles to hoist him. George means well, but he always gouges the hell out of his armpits.

Once he's on his feet, stabilizing himself with the walker, George says, "We've got to do something about this, Dad."

"Sure. I need to get out of these pajamas and get some breakfast."

"You know that's not what I'm talking about."

"I'm not going to prison."

"It's not prison. It's assisted living. You might like it." George eases him down into a chair in the kitchen. Standing behind him, George sighs and squeezes his shoulders. It's not a gesture of George's he's familiar with. Part of him wants the hands to stay there longer. Another part can't stand George hovering over him, offering help.

"I've had a long night. Let's get a little breakfast."

"These falls worry me, Dad. I don't like you staying alone like this."

He reaches up and pats George's hand. "It's okay. I'm okay." He wishes he could tell George that he worries about him too, but he'd probably upset George if he told him that. He'd take it as a criticism. He'd criticized the kids too much; maybe not more than a lot of parents, but still too much. He wishes he could take all that back now. It's probably too late. It was always too late by the time you realized things.

George is already moving away, taking another seat at the

kitchen table, and for a moment Ed sees them all in his mind, gathered once more, Lois, and George and Frank and Sis as kids.

George's voice brings him back and he wonders if he's just loopy from the fall.

"I'm serious, Dad. Let's talk about our options."

"I've had a long night, George. Let's just get a little breakfast and talk about it then."

"Good. We need to."

And there would be a way of talking about it, and nodding his head, and maybe he'd have the same kind of distant look Dickey had that night at dinner because the days ahead were short now, and it was important to remember certain things. He wishes now he'd talked more with Lois about that day and about the thoughts he'd had in the jungle about how there might be more in life for him, some other kind of future awaiting. But at least they'd finally made it to Paris. They'd taken that trip to New York too, just before Lois got sick. They'd seen *Camelot*. It was even better than the opera. Later, in the hotel room, they'd talked about it for hours, and for weeks back in Houston he'd come out of the shower singing, making Lois laugh. That great laugh. Nobody could laugh like Lois.

If he had another chance, he'd tell her of the way he came close to leaving Dickey behind. Maybe he'd even tell her about the dreams he'd had later where Mart was waking up in the jeep, his hand reaching for help.

Maybe he'd talk more to George, ask him to write some of his memories down. Maybe it wouldn't do anybody any good now— not Dickey, not Mart—for him to remember, but maybe he owed them something, some final memory of them.

He even wanted to remember the Japanese soldier, the boots guy. He was glad he hadn't had to kill him. He hoped the guy made it out of the jungle somehow, went on to live a decent life, with a wife and kids and a car in the garage, or whatever it was he wanted.

Maybe he'd tell George about the way they'd made room in the back of one of the jeeps and the way it felt as the jeep bounced over the pitted road and sent shudders through him, all up and down his spine. He'd gotten bruised up a lot over the course of the day. Things felt like shit all over his body. In the darkness Dickey rested his head against Ed's shoulder. It felt strange, Dickey's head on his shoulder in the back of the jeep, but he didn't move away. He felt much older then. He realized Dickey was crying quietly. He thought he should say something to Dickey, but he didn't know what.

He wished now he'd put his arm around him. He wished he'd held him for a little while, in the jeep, while Dickey cried.

The drive took a long time over the rough road, and then there were the lights of the base just ahead.

COME SEE US

THEY WERE STOPPED AT the channel waiting for the draw-bridge to allow a sailboat to pass under. Jenny was worried they would be late for dinner, but Tim hoped that the drawbridge would stay up so long that they could skip dinner and go back to the apartment and settle in for the night. He liked it when it was just the two of them.

He didn't like going to dinner with people he didn't know well, but Jenny said she felt obligated because she rented office space from Al and Margie. They had been invited several times and she couldn't just keep turning them down. They'd given her a very good, affordable deal, and with rents so high, she wouldn't want to offend them. For once, instead of lugging her heavy massage table from house to house, she had a fixed location and she was starting to advertise and business was picking up. Since Tim was only teaching part-time at the community college they needed to bring in more income, especially since they were thinking of starting a family. So she really needed to stay on their good side, and besides, they'd been very nice to her and she didn't want to hurt their feel-ings.

Margie and Al owned a locksmith shop. Down a short gravel driveway from the shop there was a small secondary building that had been a garage at one point, but it had been converted into a studio containing a bathroom and a wide room where she set up her table and a small desk, which they provided, and a couple of chairs. Margie and Al said they'd put a lot of effort into creating a nice space and while they weren't requiring a contract, they said they hoped she would give them proper notice. The last person in the office had left abruptly. It wasn't so much that they were upset about the rent, but they had wanted some kind of closure. People shouldn't just walk out on them.

"They're a little touchy about that sort of thing. They're very friendly, but they get hurt easily," Jenny said. Tim had met Al and Margie when Jenny was moving into the studio. They were a tanned, fit couple, Al with dark hair and Margie blonde, both in their late thirties, ten years older than Tim and Jenny. Margie had hugged him in greeting and Al insisted on helping carry things into the studio, repeatedly patting Tim on the back as if they were great friends and putting his arm around Jenny's shoulders and snugging her close. The whole time Al and Margie laughed loudly for no reason. He didn't look forward to spending more time with them.

But there was no reprieve. Within a few minutes the bridge lowered. The last evening light had faded as they drove into the main part of town, through a section of light industry, shops and a couple of cafes and Al and Margie's locksmith shop where a security light was on. Their house was a couple of miles past the shop.

"I hope we don't have to stay there too long." As on most weekends he had papers to grade and he didn't want to go into Saturday morning tired out. He had a week to go until spring break and Jenny had said maybe they should go visit her parents then, and he didn't think much of the idea. They'd spent their first year of marriage in her hometown and her parents had been nice but intrusive, making job suggestions, already hinting about grandchildren. In their second year of marriage now and living in a different state, he felt much happier. He liked living on the California coast. They had a pleasant apartment on the ground floor and a sliding glass door that opened onto a grassy courtyard. "Can we just have dinner and leave early?"

"Why is it you always worry about leaving before we even arrive?"

They passed into a suburban neighborhood and after a series of turns they arrived at a ranch-style stucco home. Tim pulled into the driveway, took a few deep breaths before exiting the car, and before they'd even reached the front door Al and Margie were already coming out, both of them wearing slacks and flowery shirts. Margie's blouse was cut low, her breasts on the verge of falling free. They were laughing riotously, carrying drinks which they forced on Tim and Jenny, hugging and kissing them, drinks sloshing. As they passed into the entryway Al lingered behind a moment to turn a lock.

The drinks were strong, already hitting him as the homeowners gave a tour of their house, pointing out some fine carpentry work Al had done here and there. Tim had no eye for such detail, but he gave appreciative comments. Al bounced exuberantly up and down on his toes and boomed, "I don't work on just locks, buddy! I can fix anything!" As if to demonstrate, he led them into a two-car garage. Two gleaming Fords of the same green color were parked side by side and tools of every variety hung neatly from hooks above the work bench and well-organized, labeled shelves lined the walls.

"Al's done everything!" Margie shrieked. "Plumbing, gutters, cars . . ."

Al nodded seriously. He put his arm around Tim's shoulder. "From now on, bring your car here. When you pulled in it sounded a little tinny. Hondas are like that. Personally, I prefer American, but bring it to me. Don't go to a shop. They'll rip you off. I'll charge you parts and a case of beer and we'll go under the hood together."

"You really do fix everything," Jenny said. There was a note of awe in her voice, which Tim found grating.

Margie shouted, "He does electrical too!"

Al whistled low. "Well, I'm backing off from electrical a little."

"Oh, Al, that fire wasn't your fault," Margie said.

"No, but maybe I'll leave that off the resume . . . And no more high-up stuff."

"Al," Marge said quietly. There was a note of warning in her voice. "You sure you want to go there, honey?"

Al swallowed, stared into space. "No. That's for late-night talk. We need more drinks for that one."

They went back into the house, refilled drinks in the kitchen, and by the time they walked into a hallway leading to the bedrooms, Al and Margie were in good spirits and laughing again. Al paused before a painting of a bowl of fruit and said, winking mysteriously, "I've got something to show you later."

"Oh, yes," Margie said. "Al's always got to show off his little toy."

Al and Margie laughed like conspirators and led them outside to a patio. There were some half-lit charcoal briquets in a grill and shish kebabs marinating on a side table. They sat on lawn chairs in a semicircle. They looked out on a small back yard with a cedar fence separating the yard from the neighbors behind and to the side. Bushes rose up high against the fence, further isolating them from the neighbors.

"You have a lot of privacy," Tim said.

Al nodded rather grimly. "It wasn't always like that."

"We used to be friends with the neighbors. We tried to be nice," Margie said. "But it didn't work out. Some people don't appreciate anything."

"We're in no rush to eat, are we?" Al said. "Let's just kick back and enjoy the evening. Se la vi, or something like that, however you say it."

"We're in no rush for anything," Marge said. "Let it all just happen. What will be will be."

Al stopped laughing. "I love this woman." He looked at Margie. "You know I love you," he said.

"I know you do, honey."

"You see," he said to Tim and Jenny. "Whatever happens between us, the four of us, we're solid."

Margie hopped out of her chair. "Drinks!" She grabbed Tim's wrist. "Come help me mix, Tim." She steered him inside to the kitchen. There were bottles all over the counter.

"What do you want me to make?"

She threw her head back and laughed. Her shoulders arched and her flowery shirt opened wider. She was beautifully tanned. "Whatever you want to make, honey, whatever and whenever, however you want it is fine." She ran her hand down his low back and onto his buttocks and he poured something fast and beelined back to the patio with Margie following, chuckling in a cannibalistic sort of way.

When he came out on the patio Jenny was still sitting in a lawn chair and Al was kneeling in front of her. Her shoes were off and her slacks were rolled up to her knee. His hands were pawing her calves, which were firm and well-shaped from her kick-boxing classes. "What the hell," Tim said.

Al looked over his shoulder. "She said she had a headache. I'm doing a little reflexology on her."

"You do reflexology?"

"I took a course."

"He has a nice touch," Jenny said.

Al laughed. "Coming from a pro, that's a high compliment. We can trade off. I'm going to come to the studio one day and get a massage from you."

Margie laughed and lifted her breasts toward the sky, "Hooboy," she said. "We won't get much work done *that* day."

Jenny made a little kicking motion and Al moved back. He sat in his chair again, on the edge. He leaned his elbows on his knees, a drink back in his hand. He stared at Jenny. "Are you happy with your studio?"

"I love it."

He nodded, rolled his tongue against his cheek as if clearing food from a molar. "That's good. Because we love you having it. You probably wonder why we gave it to you for so cheap. We could rent that out for double."

"Triple," Margie said.

"That's right," Al said. "But when you showed up to check out the space, looking so bright, so optimistic, we both knew right then. You had that something. It's hard to define. It's that something that makes the people around you better. We looked at each other and we said you're the one. You're the one we want in there. That's how we make decisions. We don't base it on money; we base it on love. And when we met Tim, honestly, we weren't sure at first. We didn't know if you were right for each other. But I can see it now. I can see the connection. We're all connected now. You're . . . you're like family already. I probably shouldn't say that."

"He means it," Margie said. "Some people think Al rushes things, but he means it."

"I say what's in my heart. Sometimes I get hurt that way. I have a full heart. I didn't always have a full heart."

"You do now," Margie said solemnly.

He grinned wide. "I love this woman." He stood up. "Margarita time."

Al went through the sliding glass door into the house.

Margie didn't look so friendly now. She was eying them both in a hardened sort of way. "What do you people want?"

"What do you mean?" Jenny asked.

"What do you want out of life? How do you want to spend your lives? How old are you?"

"Tim's twenty-eight, I'm twenty-seven."

"This is it, you know. The next ten years determines it all pretty much; where you'll be in life. You've got to make the right choices. Do you want children?"

"At some point. Probably."

"Better be sure about that, honey." She took a long swallow of her drink. "Al had a first wife," she said, talking low. "She was trouble. She never understood Al, what makes him tick. She had a wild child from a different marriage. Al looked at the world in a darker way back then. We met at an AA meeting and it just took. We realized that we didn't have that big a problem with alcohol. We blow off a little steam on Fridays and Saturdays, taper back on Sundays, and we're as sober as a judge come Monday, back to the shop and ready to work, sober as a judge."

Al appeared with a pitcher filled with drink and ice. He coughed and said, "Sober as a judge, all right. Of course, I've *known* a few judges." Al and Margie shook their heads and broke into giddy laughter.

Al poured drinks, sank into his seat. Margie leaned forward. "Tell them what you found out about yourself, Al. So they'll understand."

"Whoo-boy," Al said. He pulled back his shoulders as if widening his lungs. "You see it all. People let you into their homes. You see the bad stuff, the clutter, the plugged toilets. Some people live like shit. There are foreigners who don't speak English. It made me bitter. So I was in therapy one day and the therapist says, don't you find it ironic . . .—ironic, that's the word she used—that you're a locksmith . . . because don't you . . ." Al's voice broke. "Lock your feelings up . . . God, it just hit me. It was a dam breaking. I sobbed on her couch like a baby. I shook and I sobbed . . . It all started to change then. We found our calling. Now we find joy in everything we do. People want security, we give them security, but the real joy is when people want *in*. That's when the juices flow. They're locked out, out of their house, out of their car. They beat on the windows like babies and we say, easy now, easy, we're going to find a way back *in*." His voice trailed off. "But sometimes you've got to *keep* them in."

"Al, honey, do you want to go there?" Margie asked.

Al frowned at the marinating shish kebabs. "I'll throw these on now."

As the meat cooked they sat in a dim patio light. Tim got up and turned the shish kebabs now and then. There wasn't much heat in the coals.

Al was lapsing into his serious voice again. "There's room for a small pool out here. I think come summer we'll build a pool and we'll have you over. You need a nice place to relax."

"We have a nice courtyard where we live," Tim said.

"Well, sure. But this is ours. It's an oasis. It's yours for the asking. We know you're broke kids, fuck all to your names. But come through that front door and you're as good as any American. Be who you are. Wear clothes if you want, don't wear them if you don't. We spend whole weekends without a strip of clothing. We roll around on the carpet if we want. We don't get the government in here fucking up things, telling you what you can do, not do, taxing the shit out of every dollar you make, and giving you what? Fuck all." He slammed his fist down on the arm of his chair. "Welfare for foreigners and drug addicts."

"Al, honey, you're getting intense. You're making them nervous."

He sloshed ice around in his drink. "Bad things happen in the world. You asked about that high-up work. We were up on the fifteenth floor, Jim and me. The scaffolding broke, tilted. Jim wasn't hitched in right. He hung onto my leg. He was trying to crawl up my leg. I tried to get a line to him. If he'd held on two more seconds maybe, two more seconds . . ."

Jenny put her hands to her mouth. "Oh my God."

"No more high-up stuff. When you get a house of your own I'll come by and paint it, but I won't go up past the second story. If you've got three stories, I won't do it. I'm not afraid of many things, but I won't do heights anymore." He stared into space. "I still hear that scream. It was like the scream became part of the wind."

He frowned. "When the hell is that meat going to be ready?" He jiggled ice around in his glass. "I heard Margie mentioning my child."

Margie asked, "Are you sure you want to go there, Al?"

He nodded grimly.

"He's going there," Margie said.

"I inherited this kid. From my first wife. We lived in Arizona then. He was eleven when I got him, and he was never right in the head. He'd had a father who was no good. The kid ran around the house like a maniac. He broke things on purpose. He wouldn't stand correction. By the time he was thirteen he started slipping out at night. We weren't far from the desert. He'd come back with cactus needles in his ass. I put up locks that couldn't be turned without a key. I put bars on the windows. That held him for a while. But one night he got out again."

Jenny's voice trembled. "What happened?"

"We never knew. The police found a camp in the desert that looked like people had been squatting there. Maybe he went with them. He's probably dead or sold into some sex traffic ring."

"My God," Jenny said.

"Tell you a little secret of the trade. Best lock in the world won't keep a determined person in or a determined bad guy out. But there's something you can do about the bad guy coming in."

Margie stood up. "You've got to see this," she said.

Al led them to the hallway to the fruit bowl painting. He lifted it, set it down in the hallway. There was a nook behind the painting and in the nook sat a gray metal box. Al picked it up, carried it down the hallway to a bedroom as they followed. He set the box down on the bed and opened, it, pulled aside a soft red cloth and drew out a pistol. He turned it in his hands, staring at it with pride.

"If the bad guy breaks in and tries to diddle Margie, I blow his cojones off."

He held the gun out toward Tim. "Do you like guns?"

"I had a pellet gun as a kid."

"If we're going to hang out, you need to know about guns. Here, hold it."

"Is it loaded?'

Al chuckled. "If a bad guy breaks in, it's not going to do me much good if it's not loaded. What am I going to do? Throw it at him? Here, hold it."

"That's okay."

"Hold it. The safety's on."

Tim turned it around in his hands as if holding a bomb. "Nice," he said. He passed it back.

Al laughed. "Nice! You won't think it's so nice when I blow a hole through you." He tapped the barrel of the gun against Tim's chest. "I don't mean *you*—just whoever. This is just one of my toys. I got a whole warehouse we need to check out."

"Maybe you should put it away now," Jenny said.

"*What?*" He stopped laughing.

"I don't think they like guns, honey," Margie said.

"I'd better put it away then, before we scare the kids." He put the gun back in the nook, placed the painting over it. "Is that goddamn meat cooked yet?"

They ate on the patio at a round table. Margie brought out a wilted salad. There was no laughing now. Al made loud chewing noises. Barbecue sauce smeared his chin. His eyes closed and his head fell forward before it snapped back up. He held a kebab up and glared at it. "Who the fuck cooked this?"

When they were finished they went back inside to the den. Al and Margie sat on a couch and Al patted the couch for them to sit down. He picked up the TV controller. "I could put on a porn movie."

"No, thanks," Jenny said.

"Sorry," Tim said. "We need to get going. I have to grade papers in the morning."

Al's eyes widened as if surprised to find people in his den. He took a deep breath as if to speak, then slumped over and passed out on the arm of the couch. Jenny excused herself and went to the restroom.

"Alone at last," Margie said. She smiled at him and loosened her blouse.

Jenny came back in the room and stared at Margie's opened blouse. "What the hell," she said. Tim stood and grabbed her wrist. "We've got to go. Thanks for dinner!"

"You can't leave just like that!" Margie screamed. "How dare you!" As they ran into the darkened entryway, she went into the hall. She was moving the painting, reaching into the nook. Tim twisted the lower knob and shook the door, but it wouldn't open without a key to turn the upper lock. Margie came back into the dark entryway, her hand holding something shiny. They pinned themselves against the door, huddled together. "Let's rush her," Jenny whispered.

"Move aside," Margie ordered.

She wasn't holding a gun, but a keychain. She turned the lock and opened the door and as they ran onto the lawn, Al stumbled through the front door, demanding, "Why are they leaving?"

"We'll see you Monday!" Margie called.

Al grabbed hold of Jenny's shirt. She brought her knee up and kicked backward, sticking her heel into his stomach. He grunted and fell back on the grass and Margie bent over him. "Al, honey, are you okay?"

He flung his arm up. "Help me! God, help me!"

They got in the car and locked the doors. They didn't discuss it but they both knew. He drove to the locksmith shop and down the gravel driveway and they loaded up her massage table and her other belongings.

Jenny glanced once over her shoulder as they drove away. "It was such a sweet little studio."

"We'll find you another one."

"I should give notice."

"We'll send them next month's rent. That will be notice enough."

The drawbridge was up again as a boat passed through the channel. It was dark and quiet inside the car. No one was in line behind them. The air outside had chilled, and he put the heater on. It made a faint, tinny, rattling sound.

"Tell me our child won't be a wild child," Jenny said.

"Our child won't be a wild child."

"And we'll never be like them."

"We'll never be like them. We'll be our own people. We'll make our own way."

The drawbridge lowered and they drove on.

HEADING FOR SHORE

JAILER DAN GATHERED US, the twenty or so newbies, in the dirt in front of the prison building. There wasn't even a fence around the prison yard, and we could see the ocean not far away, but we couldn't see to the mainland. Dan didn't have a gun or a nightstick on his hip and we didn't see any guards around. He smiled as if he'd read our minds.

"That's right, boys," he said. "You'll hardly even notice the guards around here. We think of them more as facilitators than guards. They'll keep you fed—three squares a day, damn good cuisine if I say so myself. Snack time. Cookies and milk. You'll have a hard time not getting fat."

Spiff raised his hand, his voice shaking a little. "What about our meds, Boss?"

Dan chuckled. "You don't need to worry about that. We personalize it. You'll all get the right mix. What else do you need?"

Spiff sniffled. "I want a garden with some tomato plants."

Dan chuckled. "Sure, you can have a garden with some tomato plants. Why not?"

Clyde was a big, hard-looking fellow. "How far to the mainland?"

Dan beamed. "Five miles. Bad currents. Sharks up your ass. You don't want to even think ocean unless you're a Navy Seal."

Clyde cleared his throat. "Well, I am a Navy Seal," he said. "Seven years."

"Me too," Big Jim said. He was standing next to Clyde.

"Fuck the sharks," Clyde said.

Jailer Dan wasn't chuckling now. "Come on, boys. Don't talk that way." He spread his legs like a cheerful coach. "The boys are waiting in the building."

Dan waved toward the building and hands came through the bars and waved back. "The guys are looking forward to meeting you. They cooked up one hell of a lasagna."

Clyde and Big Jim looked at each other. "Think I'll go for a swim. What about you, Jim?"

Big Jim nodded. "Let's blow this joint."

Dan patted his hip, frowned, as if becoming aware there was no gun there. "Now come on, guys, *come on!* Play nice. What about your friends? They can't swim like you."

The lawyer stepped forward. "Why don't we just take a boat?"

Dan's lips twitched. "A boat?"

"Sure, I Googled this place. There's a dock on the east side of the island. We'll just walk over there and get a boat."

Dan sputtered. "They're not nice over there. Look, guys, you're getting the wrong idea about this place. Let's go inside and eat lasagna."

"We get the idea, all right," the lawyer said. "You get us in there and we never get out."

"You won't *want* to get out. Once you see what we have to offer."

"*Exactly,*" the lawyer said. "I'm heading for the boat."

"Now, come on. Don't do this. You're going to screw up the system for everybody."

"Shut up," Clyde said, "before we lay beaters on you. Let's go, boys."

Dan was sweating. "Think about it. Three squares, meds. Cookies."

We started walking, following Clyde and Big Jim and the lawyer. Jailer Dan was trailing along, whispering to some of the guys, and their shoulders tilted as they walked, as if a wind was blowing them back. They began to peel off, to fall behind, to lag off toward the building where the guys waved from the windows. Spiff's shoulders sagged, but he kept walking beside me, step by step, and I touched his back to tell him it would be okay, though I wasn't so sure. We walked across the island, what was left of us; less than half. The sun was shining and it felt good to move our legs. There was no one around at the dock. Clyde and Big Jim unhitched a small fishing boat and we boarded. We crossed a choppy sea, raising our heads to the sky, the spray of water on our cheeks. When we got to land we all shook hands, had sort of a group hug. Some of us had tears in our eyes. Clyde and Big Jim laughed and fell on the shore and grappled and tried to pin each other. Then we went our own ways.

The years roll by. Sure, bad things happened to some of the guys. Maybe they didn't belong on the mainland. But some of us did okay. I'm married now, got kids, a steady job. I'm a regular guy now. I wake up and shave. We've got a garden with some tomato plants. If I saw Spiff again, I'd say: Come stay with us. Come sit in our garden with the tomato plants. The years roll by. People, friends, they scatter to the four winds. I'll catch up with some of you sometime.

THE PROBLEM YOU HAVE

I DRANK WAY TOO much in high school and then college, and just after college I took a trip to Mexico.

The trip turned into a year. I got a job at a language school teaching English in the evenings in the next town over from where I was living. The school used audiotapes with British actors, so our students spoke in a rather melodious mix of Mexican and British accents. The Director, Jack, was a skinny, red-headed guy from New York. He was thirty-two, ten years older than me, and he was always eager to divulge unwanted personal information. If I bumped into Jack in the front office or in one of the corridors of the small school or encountered him in the flowery courtyard with the fountain and goldfish pond, he might take me aside to report on something he found fascinating, like his latest epic bowel movement.

"Wow," I might say. I said "wow" a lot in those days.

Most of the students were secretaries or lower-level managers, sent by their companies to the school. One of the former students was married to Jack. Sondra was my age, beautiful, slender, dark-haired with stunningly clear brown eyes.

At first it was a safe, poetic sort of attraction, which I assumed was doomed to come to nothing. I'd been raised Catholic, and though I rarely went to mass anymore, I liked to sit in churches when they were empty and messages would come about leaving married women alone. One voice I kept hearing in my mind was my old Texas friend cowboy Mike, saying, "Get your shit together, boy. Leave that girl alone."

One evening in the school office, just before our classes, Jack gestured toward the large wooden desk. It was mostly bare except for a big black telephone and some file folders. "I fucked Sondra on that desk last night after we closed up school," he said.

I shook my head as if I were clearing water out of my ears. I turned my head sideways to observe the desk from a different angle. "Wow," I said.

A couple of nights later I found myself alone in the office with Sondra. No longer attending classes herself, she played an administrative role. She glanced at the desk and looked sad and contemplative. She gave me a quizzical look. Suddenly there was a silence between us, and I sensed that she knew of my own desire for her. She was not exactly either pleased or disturbed by the realization, but maybe a little amused. Still, we had formed a small bond. Jack came into the office. "I just pissed for a full five minutes," he said. "It kept coming and coming. I had to tighten my ass muscles to slow it down."

My eyes lifted wide, but I did not say wow. Sondra backed up against the desk and stared with a kind of dread, as if he might suddenly erupt in front of us.

In the following months I found my whimsical love was growing stronger. Sometimes I thought about speaking to her, of saying something along the lines of *Sondra, you've made a big mistake. Your husband is a lout.* I wouldn't expect her to go off with me right away, on the spot. But maybe she'd become haunted by the idea of running away with me. Did she really want to spend her life with a guy who described his own turds?

Sondra was quiet and shy, and her eyes held a light and shine when she'd lift her chin and stare at me. I noticed that about people's eyes. A lot of people have dead eyes, as if their spirits, too, have died. Sometimes my own eyes went dead when I drank too much, but they would come back alive if I stayed off the booze for a few days. Her eyes reminded me of lights sparking out of a cave. I wrote a bad poem about it, in fact, titled "Lights Sparking Out of a Cave." I wrote it on a napkin when I was in a bar, and I lost the poem and could only remember the first line, which repeated the title, "Her eyes are like lights sparking out of a cave," so I didn't really have much of a poem.

As time went on the light in Sondra's eyes was dimming. I had a growing sense that she was unhappy with Jack. One night I noticed a blemish to the side of her left eye, a darkish bruising. She'd put makeup on it, but it showed when we were alone in the office with the light above the desk.

She saw me looking at the bruise and she gave one of her little laughs, though it did not contain any amusement. "It's nothing," she said. "I fell. It's nada."

"Nada, pues nada," I said, an allusion to a Hemingway story I'd shared with her.

Recognizing the reference, this drew a more genuine laugh and a flash of light in her eyes.

Jack came in off the courtyard and he looked at us, his face tightening as if he were in pain. He held his hand out to me. "Pull my thumb," he said. "Pull it quick. My thumb is out of joint."

I took hold of his thumb and pulled. His face squinched up with effort and he let out an explosive fart that made me take a step back. "Ah," he sighed. His lips stretched mirthfully wide.

I made silent laughing motions with my mouth in the way one does when he is playing along with a dumb joke, but I was disturbed by the bruise on Sondra's cheek, so my response was more measured than he might have liked. "Fuck you all if you can't take a joke," he said and went off chuckling into the courtyard.

"I should have warned you," Sondra said. "He loves that joke."

"It's a good one," I said, rolling my eyes. She sighed as if acknowledging Jack's crudeness but trying to bear it. She startled me then. She put two fingers to her lips, kissed them, reached out and touched not my lips but my nose. She giggled at my surprise. "Go teach. Teach them the pluperfect," she said, alluding to another of our inside jokes stemming from the time I had revealed that I actually did not know the name of many of the verb tenses. "I would if I knew what it was," I said and she took me by the shoulders and gave me a little push in the back, the way a coach might send a favorite player onto the field. I left the office with trembling legs, crossed the flowery courtyard with the fountain, a tropical bird squawking at me from a tree, and when I entered the classroom my students greeted me cheerfully and I wobbled before them, their faces blurring in the suddenly too bright light.

Voices came at me. "Hallo, Dave. How are you? Are you well today?"

I gave my head a shake and their faces came back into focus, particularized so that I could see the students as individuals again. "Thank you. I am very well."

Roberto, always eager, from the front of the room inquired, "Would you like some fish?"

I remembered we had been working on a food and restaurant unit at the last class. I smiled. "Yes, I would very much like some fish. What kind of fish do you have?"

"Oh," Roberto said. "We have . . ." He looked about the room for help.

Maria, from the side of the room, came to his aid. "We have a big fish. You want a big fish?"

"Yes, I would like a big fish."

Yeah, I'd like a big fish to pull to shore like old Ernie Hemingway. But I kept thinking about the way Sondra's fingers touched my nose.

As the days went by I began to think more about my nose. I hadn't really thought much about my nose before the kiss of her fingers, but now when I looked at it in the mirror I noticed the slight curve in it. My older brother had broken my nose once, not meaning to, only meaning to hit me in a friendly sort of way. But if my nose was a bit crooked, it felt blessed after that touch. Would every part of me that Sondra touched feel blessed?

I taught evenings from five to nine Mondays, Wednesday, and Fridays. The city I taught in was over an hour away by bus from where I lived, so I needed to catch the 3:00 p.m. bus to make it on time. There was a three-thirty bus if I missed the first one, but if I took the later one, after the ride and the twenty-minute walk through town, I would arrive at my first class a few minutes late. At first I thought everybody was fine with this, but one evening the class gave me sullen looks and complained about my being late, so after that I always made sure to catch the 3:00 p.m. bus. It made me feel responsible to catch the bus on time and now with the blessed nose, I felt better about life than I had in a long time. I was hardly drinking at all, and I was feeling overall well and sane.

In the months before this newfound sobriety came over me, I had been going out to bars every night. Before I went out to the bars I left myself two sandwiches on the kitchen table in my apartment, along with a piece of paper and a pen. When I came home my intention was to eat the two sandwiches, which would help reduce my hangover in the morning, and I was to write myself a note, something along the lines of: *You were fine tonight, you insulted no one, you got in no fights, no one is angry at you.* I wrote myself a note because I knew that when I woke up in the morning I was likely not to remember parts of the night. But if I woke up and found the note and saw that I had eaten the sandwiches, I would know that I had arrived home in reasonable shape, even if I didn't remember all that had occurred. It was when I didn't find the note or saw that I hadn't eaten the sandwiches that I became alarmed.

I thought of quitting drinking, but mostly I thought of somehow controlling it. What was most disturbing was the blackouts. If I could simply quit having the blackouts, I would be okay. To entirely give up drinking seemed extreme and rather impossible under the circumstances. That is, before I fell in love with Sondra.

When I'd first arrived in the Mexican town, which I will not name for legal purposes, I'd met a peg-legged man who had introduced himself as some type of real estate agent. I followed the peg-legged man through the cobblestone streets, looking for a place to live.

I spoke little Spanish, but Juan was fluent in English. He had almost no accent, though his phrasing was a little stiff. We stood in front of an electrical or mechanical shop—there were several men in a dark shop who wore safety goggles and machinery was whirling away and there were sounds of hammering and electrical sawing and sparks flew from work tables and there was the odor of something metallic burning and there were glimmers in the background of silvery and coppery materials being worked into shape and then a man cursing and waving his hand in the air as if he'd just severed a finger or pounded it in a painful way, but after a moment or two of waving his hand through the air the man resigned himself and once more bent over the work table.

A man with a mustache wearing a work apron came out of the dimness and he looked at the peg-legged man in a knowing way, as if it were all already arranged. The man beamed at me, and Juan communicated between us. The man went back into the shop and brought out a set of keys and tried several on the red door next to the shop until one finally worked. I went upstairs with Juan, but the man in the work apron stayed behind.

There was a big room looking out on the street and across the narrow street there was another house much like this one, a white stucco house with a small balcony. That house had potted flowers on the balcony wall, and I thought I might like to get some potted flowers myself. Behind the big room there was a kitchen, and then there was an outdoor patio space. I would need to walk across the outdoor space to reach the bathroom and the shower. It was fall, not really cold, but at this high altitude it was on the chilly side in the morning, and I thought that it would be okay, rather bracing, to cross the patio. I flicked on the light switch in the bathroom and no light came on. It was a small bathroom, though it did have, in a very condensed space, a toilet, a sink, and a shower.

"There's no light in there," I told Juan.

Juan shook his head at the small matter. "Only until tonight. Tonight there will be electricity in all the house."

"Oh, you mean there is no electricity inside the house either?"

"Tonight," Juan said. "Tonight there will be electricity."

"You're sure?"

"The shop below is all about electricity."

We went below. The man with the apron met us on the sidewalk and he and Juan spoke. Juan turned to me and said, "He says there will be electricity tonight, and hot water."

I did like the place. I could see myself sitting on the patio on sunny days. "Okay, sure," I said.

Though the shop below was all about electricity, there was, in fact, no electricity at all for another week, and after that it would go off suddenly. After a while I got used to the apartment with intermittent electricity. It had become something of a joke between the landlord and me. Encountering him, I might say with a comical arch of my eyebrows, "¿La electricidad?" Always the same beaming promise: "¡Esta noche!"

When the electricity was off I lit candles. I also kept a flashlight handy on the kitchen table where the two sandwiches would be waiting. There were some mornings when I woke up in bed, still wearing my shoes, my clothing disheveled, and I'd stumble into the kitchen holding my pounding head, discover the sandwiches were still uneaten on the table, then search my memory with dread, wondering if I had gotten in any fights or insulted anyone or acted inappropriately.

Many years later I would think of all this as strange and erratic behavior, and even then, at clearer headed moments, I viewed my behavior as reckless, unworthy, unredeemable. At the same time, though, it was exhilarating to be young and living in Mexico, writing a poem from time to time.

Much of my bad behavior, the heavy drinking, had occurred before I got close to Sondra. In recent months I had been staying mostly sober because of her, because of my desire to be her knight, to protect her from the dragon, Jack. But fiesta time was coming around again, and I worried about the temptations.

But at the same time, in my newfound sobriety, I had a heightened sense of awareness that was almost like insanity. Looking back I see flashes of myself, going in and of classrooms, crossing paths with Sondra, with Jack. A few other teachers were there at times, but I only had brief contact with them, and they did not make much of an impression on me. It seemed to always be Sondra, Jack, me, five to nine, four one-hour classes right after another with brief breaks between.

Jack and Sondra lived in the same town as I did, and they took a van over earlier in the day, so I did not ride to work with them. There were some nights when I drove home with them, but they often stayed late to close up the school, so I usually preferred to catch the bus, and, besides, now I was worried that Jack might try to make love with Sondra on the big desk while I was waiting in the courtyard. I think he would have enjoyed having me listen. He delighted in the jealousy he had detected in me.

On some nights Sondra didn't come over from the other town and on some of those nights Jack was ready to leave earlier, so I sometimes took a ride with him in his red van, though I knew those rides were likely to bring more unwanted revelations. He enjoyed talking about his past. He'd been in the navy at one point, but they'd thrown him out for lewd conduct (big surprise there!). He'd worked in the Midwest as a traveling salesman. He'd sold subscriptions to magazines and great books—one could buy a great book each month. He'd driven about in Iowa and Nebraska selling the magazine and great book subscriptions. "I never made much money at it," he said one night as our headlights flickered eerily over rough scrub land dotted with mesquite trees, "but it was great driving down country roads with this girl I met in Omaha. She gave the best blow jobs I've ever had. One time I ran off the road, but she never let up the whole time. Sondra doesn't like giving head. She licks at it like it's something diseased."

"Hey, Jack, okay, enough. *Enough!*"

He also liked telling me about his mob connections back in New York. He gave the impression that he was privy to some really bad stuff, gang shootings, snitches dropped in rivers, things along those lines. But then, as if fearing maybe he'd gone too far, he'd wave his hand in a gesture of innocence. "Hey, everybody in New York hears about those kinds of things." But a moment later there would be a kind of winking innuendo that maybe, just maybe, he had a little more intimate knowledge. One night he admitted that he had a gun, a definite no-no for an American in Mexico. He carried it in the van in case of banditos on the road. He gave me a kind of curious, sidelong glance. "Or if anyone messes with Sondra."

So there were more reasons for me now not to ride in the van, as I didn't want anything to do with the gun, but one night there was a cold rain that I would have to walk through to the bus stop. Sondra was there that night and I knew Jack would tone it down some with her onboard, so when they offered to close up early and give me a ride I accepted, also in part because it was September again, the month of fiestas, so I thought it might be nice to get back to town earlier and go out if the rain stopped

We drove through the city, past the Pemex station, and I felt a curious sense of forlornness as we left the last town buildings behind and set out down a dark, narrow road that would stretch ahead for forty miles before we came to the welcoming lights of the town where we lived. I hoped that I would have electricity tonight, as the thought of a dark apartment did not appeal to me, but there was, of course, the fiesta. Maybe, after all, it was time to get drunk again. The situation with Sondra was hopeless. Why remain in this sort of stoical solitude?

I was in the back and it was dark and the rain was coming down hard, nearly blinding our view of the road ahead, and we had all fallen silent, all of us straining forward when a man appeared in the headlights. I glimpsed a sombrero and a yellow-looking face turning toward the headlights, an arm raising to shield himself. Sondra screamed, "Jack!"

He swung the wheel hard to the left. We heard a thump and Jack drove on a little and stopped on the side of the road and said, in a dull voice, "Maybe it was just a dog."

Sondra said, as if to a child, "It wasn't a dog, Jack."

"I'll check," I said.

"Don't get out," Jack said, still in that same dull voice. "It could be a trap."

But I slid open the side door and got out. I went back along the shoulder of the road. I couldn't see in the darkness, but I kept moving until my feet hit something. I bent over. I was touching around on his back, as if I might be able to wake him. The van swung back around, did a U-turn, and the headlights illuminated us, the man on the ground as I stood over him, touching his shoulder. He wasn't dead, but he wasn't conscious. His feet were kicking lightly in the gravel to the side of the road and there was a terrible flow of blood coming out of his head and mouth. I turned away and bent over, dry heaving.

When I stood back upright, Jack stood beside me and we looked at the man's booted toes paw the gravel.

"We've got to get him in the van," I said. "We've got to take him to town."

"He's gone," Jack said. "Or he will be in a minute. We need to clear out of here. It's our ass if we report this."

"It was an accident."

"It won't matter. They'll throw our asses in jail."

"We need to help him."

Jack looked down at the man. One foot kept twitching, but the other had stopped. "Sure," Jack said. "You're right. Pull the van up."

I started running back to the van when I jumped at the blast behind me. I was frozen for a moment as the gunshot rang through the air. Then I turned and ran back toward Jack and the man on the ground. Jack walked back toward me, gun in his hand, his face wild in the headlights.

"What did you do?" I screamed.

He pointed the gun at my head. "Get in the van. Get in the fucking van!"

Numb, I got back in the van. As Jack drove, Sondra was crumpled against the door crying.

When Jack spoke, his voice was calm. "If we report this, we'll all spend years in a Mexican prison. You too, Dave. You're part of this now. Sondra too. Remember that."

"You shot him," Sondra said, and her voice had a strange, plaintive quality, as if all were lost now.

"I didn't shoot him," he said in an eerily calm voice. "There was a wild dog coming for him. I shot at the dog to drive it off."

Sondra covered her face with her hands, and I leaned over the seat to touch her shoulder. We both knew then that he was crazy.

Jack parked outside my apartment, but he followed me upstairs. I didn't bother with trying the lights. I didn't want light. "Don't say anything about this to anyone," Jack said. "We needed to clear out of there, so I put him out of his pain, that's all." He added then, absurdly, "Take the rest of the week off."

I had a bottle of tequila in the apartment, and I drank in the darkness, right out of the bottle. I fell into bed. I had curious dreams and images. In one dream that seemed to go on for hours, I was at the school. Roberto was asking me if I wanted a big fish to eat. The students were talking in British accents. I had a profound sense in the dream of already missing everyone. I was like a ghost, coming and going through the flowery courtyard, the tropical bird squawking. I was searching for myself, for some past life or something, and it seemed to me in the dream that was not quite a dream that everything in my life had been about searching for some past that had never really existed, or maybe for some past person who had never really existed. Shadows, lights, an arm raised to the glare, the tropical bird squawking at me in the flowery courtyard, and Jack and I sitting beside the fountain. He had a gun in his hand hung down between his knees.

I'm not sure how much time went by, but I woke in a fright, realizing there was a knocking at the street door. My first thought was that it was the police. When I went downstairs and opened the door, Sondra was standing there. She was wearing a serape. She came in out of the rain. We didn't talk at all. I led her up the stairs. We didn't say anything. We fell into bed in the darkness. We started kissing and entwining our bodies together. I could feel the wetness of her clothes. Her body stopped moving against mine. We lay in the stillness and quiet, the rain beating down.

"I can't," she said.

We sat on the side of the bed together. "Jack's right," she said. "If we say anything, we'll all go to prison. That's the way it works here."

"Let's go away. You and me."

She was silent. Then she said, "I'm pregnant."

I sat there, taking this in. Finally, I said, "I'll help raise the baby," but there was a strain in my voice.

"What would we do? How would we live?"

"We'll figure something out."

"You need to go away," she said.

"Go where?"

"Go back to your own country."

I couldn't say anything for a while. I sat there and my head and shoulders felt enormously heavy, as if I'd already been sentenced to some terrible penalty. Finally, I looked up. "I'll come back for you. When this is all over."

"No." She shook her head. "My family will take care of me. But you can't, Dave. You can't. It would be bad for both of us. All this . . ." She waved her hand as if dismissing evil spirits. "Must go away. You must go away."

Two fingers, touching my lips. A blessing. A goodbye.

She went away. I fell back into my dreams and images and my drinking. A day or two went by. I didn't really remember going there but I found myself at the fiesta one night. People were milling around the square and spilling out of a cantina on the corner. Mariachis were playing from a gazebo in the square. The trees in the square glowed with lights and in front of the church fireworks exploded into the night and I stood and watched them, distantly, none of it meaning anything to me. I thought maybe I would work my way through the crowd and go into the church and sit there in the quiet and darkness. I would just sit there and let the stillness wash over me. Through my boozy haze I became aware that Jack was standing a few feet away from me. He had been standing there for some time watching me. Sondra wasn't with him. I opened my mouth. I formed the word "murderer." I may have said it aloud. Then he was gone in the crowd, and I was walking home down a quiet, dark cobblestone sidewalk, when the van pulled alongside me.

"Get in," he said out the driver's window.

"I wouldn't get in your van for fucking anything."

"Please," he said. "Sondra wants to talk to you. The three of us need to talk. We've decided to go to the police. We just need to tell the story right. I don't want Sondra or you to get in trouble. Come on. Do this for Sondra, will you?"

I came around the van and got into the passenger seat and when he drove on, I said, "Why did you shoot him?"

"You weren't going to let me leave him there."

"It was an accident. Until you shot him."

"The police would make our lives hell, even for an accident. It would probably be prison for that alone or they'd shake us down for every penny we own for the rest of our lives. We'd never get out of it."

"We could go back to the States."

"I've got nothing there. Nothing. Everything I have is here now. I've got the school, Sondra, the baby. I'm not losing all that. I want you to be part of us."

"What do you mean?"

He was silent for a moment, then he said, "You're in love with Sondra, aren't you?"

I didn't answer.

"Of course you are . . . What I mean is, I don't mind you having seconds."

"What?"

"She likes you a lot too. I don't mind if you fuck her now and then. We can fuck her together if you want."

"Let me out."

He drove fast. "I had to know, and I know now. One day you'll report this. Maybe not right away. But one day you will and you'll take everything away from me, just like that. It will bite you too. You're an accessory. You know the problem you have? You've got a conscience."

We were turning fast, leaving the town lights behind and heading into the countryside.

I was sobering up fast now. "Where the hell are you going?"

A few miles outside the town he pulled the van to the shoulder of the road. Open fields spread out to either side of the road. There was no traffic coming or going. It was dark inside the van, but I saw a glint of metal. He'd raised the gun up from below the driver's seat. "Get out." He wagged the gun and I got out.

"Walk" he ordered. I started walking in the darkness. "Just keep walking," he said, and I heard the break in his voice, as if this was going to be harder for him than he'd realized.

I broke into a run. I zig-zagged. The bullets whacked into the dark earth around me, but I kept running into the blackness ahead.

He yelled, "Come back! I was just trying to scare you!" I kept running, but I looked back and saw the headlights coming my way, the van bouncing over a field. There was a ravine to my left. I hoped if he kept going out across the field, I might be able to circle back and get to the road and flag down a car or truck if one came along. I turned my head, and it looked like the headlights were moving past me, but now they were swinging around in my direction. I climbed down into the ravine. I crawled under brush, hoping there wasn't a rattler in there. The van stopped and the door opened and shut.

He walked along the edge of the ravine, shining a flashlight.

"Dave," he yelled loudly, as if I might be far away. "I was just fucking with your head! Let me take you home. Don't do this, man. We're friends." He kept shining the light, then the light went back the other way. After a while I heard the van starting up and driving off. I climbed out of the ravine. The van had stopped at the shoulder of the road. A thin stab of light appeared in the darkness. He was coming on foot, intermittently shining the flashlight. I ran away from the road until I was panting. I turned to look back. The flashlight probed into the ravine where I'd hid. I kept running and each time I looked back the light was farther and farther away. Then it bobbed a little as he reversed course, back toward the road again, and after a while the headlights of the van turned about and headed in the direction of town.

I spent the night in the field near the ravine, cold and shivering. Coyotes howled in the night. At dawn I made my way back to the road. Buses in the area would stop for you alongside the road if you waved at them. I flagged one down. I left everything behind. I took three different buses, and by the next morning I was crossing over the border. But I was never quite sure he wouldn't come after me. For years, whenever I saw a red van, I wanted to take off running.

I always felt sad that I'd never said goodbye to the students or to the people who worked below in the shop. I always thought that maybe one day I'd go back there to find Sondra, to make sure she was okay. But I never did.

I still see that man, the way his arm went up before we hit him, then the blood and his feet twitching while we stood over him. Jack was wrong, though. I never reported it. Maybe I didn't have the right sort of conscience after all.

SMITTY'S ON THE MOUND

NINTH INNING AND SMITTY'S the closer. The lead-off batter connects hard on the first pitch, a fast ball that's not so fast, and Smitty takes his cap off on this sunny afternoon to cool his head and watches the ball soar all the way to the warning track before the right fielder makes a heroic leap to save the ball from going over the fence. The fielder sprawls on the ground and holds his glove up to show he's made the catch. The few fans scattered in this out-in-the-desert-end-of-the-road, bush-league stadium applaud as the fielder staggers up, shakes his head like he's received a chiropractic adjustment, throws the ball back in, and resumes his position. The fans give him another round of applause and the fielder waves and tips his hat. Hotshot, Smitty thinks. Just make the catch without all the drama.

But the near homer shakes Smitty up, gives him that slack feeling in his legs he knows too well. *Stop!* He's talked to his therapist about this, this kind of insecurity. *Think positive!* The majors are still possible. At *his* age? Who is he kidding? Washed up. Washed up without ever really getting going. *Stop!*

He walks the next three batters, throwing the ball in the dirt, to the sides, Squatty the catcher diving to stop the ball, dusting himself off, removing his face guard and banging it on his thighs to clean the dirt off, blowing out hard breaths, as if the throws have exhausted all his patience. Even the ump shakes his head and looks disgusted. That's *harsh*, Smitty thinks. Those pitches weren't so bad! Bases loaded, one out, the clueless homefield fans jeering, and now he's staring at a righty at the plate, their best hitter, standing with a wide, threatening stance, drooling at the mouth, wagging his bat, theatrically pointing to center field in a clownish Babe Ruth impression. Give me a break. We'll show *you*, Babe! Two more balls in the dirt, Squatty blocking the throws with his mitt and shin guards, barely checking the runner on third from stealing home. There's nothing Squatty hates more than a stealer. He's a short, fierce little bastard with hairy forearms.

No genius behind the plate, Squatty signals what pitch to throw. One finger, now two, now three, now a thumb and a finger. Now Squatty appears to be *shooting* the finger at him! The ump leans over Squatty, the two of them whispering to each other, and the batter turns his head and all three chuckle together.

Skipper, the head coach, has come out of the dugout, getting in on the signaling, making the sign of the cross on his chest. His hands move to his head. Something's gotten under his cap. He's scratching frantically at his skull, and he's doing some kind of tap dance, one hand in his hair, the other clutching his crotch.

The batter is getting bigger. The wagging bat itself is turning into a huge piece of lumber that's going to drive the ball right back at Smitty, knock his head off. It's like his reoccurring dream he's told the therapist about, where a line drive knocks his head off and then, blind, he's searching for his head in the infield, kicking it like a soccer ball while his father, an old marine, screams at him to throw the head to first.

Wow, that's a good one, the therapist had said. Were you afraid of your father?

He'd told him about that night when he was fourteen. In the hallway of his house, his father holding the electric clippers, telling Smitty it's time to come down to the utility room for his haircut. The old man, a good guy in many ways, gives buzz cut haircuts, the electric clippers smoking, and sends him off to school where everybody makes fun of his stubbly head. No, he tells his father this time, I'm not getting a haircut.

The old marine laughs it off at first. Oh, sure you are.

No, I'm not.

Don't be silly.

I'm not being silly. I'm not getting a haircut.

And on it goes, round and round—You're getting one; No, I'm not—until the old man's face turns red and he snarls, You say no one more time and I'm going to hit you.

I'll hit you back.

Smitty's big for fourteen. The old man looks at him and his shoulders slump and he says, Fine then. Okay, if that's the way you want it. He walks away with his clippers, like a beaten batter heading for the dugout.

Maybe they never quite got over that day. One thing can happen where you lose a lifetime of love. Maybe not the whole package, but something that taints the love, stains it, makes it never quite the same. Something that needs forgiving, but the forgiving never happened and he tells the therapist it's too late now because the old man died a few months ago.

Smitty paws at the dirt with his cleats, takes his cap off, looks at the sky, watches a plane passing in the distance. Thinks of home, his wife, Viv, a talented pole dancer. So much time on the road. What's it all about? Voices from the stands: *Throw the ball!*

Chatter from the other team's dugout; maybe from his own dugout too. Is the team turning on him? *Pitcher, pitcher, he's not a pitcher, he's a belly itcher!* Really? He hasn't heard that one since he was a kid in little league. They're not going to get to him with *that* one! But he feels strangely hurt. He's not a belly itcher. He's not!

Squatty again with those flashing fingers; Skipper screaming for him to throw.

Fast ball, curve, maybe the slider? He rears back but halfway through his delivery he can't decide on what pitch he's throwing and he lobs the ball straight up in the air, the ball coming right back down to himself on the mound, and he catches it as if he's planned it all along, some brilliant strategy, the runners on the bases too confused to move. The ump frowns. He shakes his head in reproach and calls ball three. One ball more and the runner from third comes in to tie the game and the bases will still be loaded.

The sparse crowd jeering. Smitty tries to ignore them. Lame bastards! *You* try pitching!

Skipper trots to the mound, shoulders pulled back, fists at the sides of his chest, jutting gut out in front. It's a calm trot, as if Skipper has found peace within himself, arrived at a decision which is grim but necessary. He's sending Smitty to the showers. It's the ultimate humiliation. The closer failing to close.

Squatty and the rest of the infield come in for the final consult, enclosing him as if they're doing an intervention.

Skipper holds his hand out. "Ball." He enunciates the word in a slow, meaningful way. He savors the minimalism of the phrasing. *Ball.* As if the word says it all. As if Smitty doesn't deserve the ball.

But he *does*. What did that therapist say? Take ownership. That's right. Take *ownership* of the ball. He's the closer. He's going to *close.* Nobody's taking the ball from him.

Once he explains things, Skipper will come around. "It was the signals, Skipper. I didn't know what you and Squatty were trying to tell me."

Skipper nods. "That's the problem, Smitty. You never know what people are trying to tell you."

"I just want to pitch."

"Sure, sure. We all want to pitch. Everybody wants to be a pitcher."

Again that chatter, carrying on the thin, hot, dry desert air: *He's not a pitcher, he's a belly itcher!*

Skipper frowns. "That true, Smitty? Are you a belly itcher?"

"No. *No!*"

"The thing is, Smitty," he says, nodding at the ring of players who nod somberly back, "we've all been meaning to talk to you."

"You have?"

"There's things going on with you, Smitty. You're not yourself."

"I'm not?"

"I've spoken to your wife."

"To my *wife*?"

"She told me about your ED."

"Why the hell are you talking to my wife about my ED?"

"That's the sort of thing we need to know, Smitty. You lose that, you lose the arm."

"My God. This is outrageous."

"The other thing is you're not keeping up with the research."

"The *research*?"

"What kind of pitches you got?"

"I got a lot of pitches. I got a fastball."

Squatty snorts. His face guard is tilted up on his head.

"I got a fastball, I got a curve, a slider, a knuckle ball."

"That's not much of a knuckler."

"Yeah, maybe, but the rest of them . . ." Damn right! Lots of good pitches over the years. Snaking the ball over the corner of the plate while batters swung in futility, banged their bats on the ground in despair, hung their heads, and made the long, shameful walk back to the dugout.

Pitched everywhere. But never the big one. The Grand Cabana. The Big Cheese. The Show! Hell, no, but close that time, kind of close. Double A, a shot at being called up to Triple A, then who knew? He could almost taste the money, the glory.

"The thing is, Smitty, you're not staying current in the field. There's kids coming up with all kinds of new pitches, pitches you've never even dreamed of in your philosophy, Horatio."

"What the hell are you talking about?"

"Your pitches are dated. One-dimensional. There's young guys coming up, throwing whole new stuff, the Obi One Kenobi, the hooley-booley, the thunderama, the Harry Houdini. You've slacked. You haven't kept up with the times, Smitty."

Smitty hangs his head. It's Iowa. It's Iowa again. *Don't go there!*

Muggy afternoon in late August. He's eighteen years old, trying out for the University of Iowa baseball team. He's a top prospect, got one of the best high school winning records. Sure, four years at Iowa. Build up the repertoire, maybe work on the knuckler. Then the Yankees. Yeah, the Yankees—that's the way to go. But today all they care about is speed. Can he hit the required speed limit to make the team? It's all up to the electronic timer. Nothing personal. He comes up two miles per hour too slow. The pitching coach gives him the thumb. Had your chance, now off the mound. Wait a minute here! The Yankees! What about the Yankees? Sorry, kid. You're two miles per hour too slow.

You pitch to a batter! You don't pitch to an electronic timer! But it's all gone, the dream fading. No Iowa team, no Yankees, a series of tryouts in minor leagues, riding crappy buses, eating in cheap diners, drinking in sleazy bars.

"Give me the ball, kid."

"No."

"Take some time off. Take six months. Work cn that thing with your wife."

The boys chuckle. Squatty snorts. Snot comes out his nose.

"Strike out in a new direction." Skipper lifts his cap, lets air in and puts it back on. He adjusts the crotch of his uniform. "Strike out. I didn't mean to say it that way, but if you ever struck anybody out anymore, maybe we wouldn't be having this conversation. How do you tell a guy he's through? What tactful way is there of saying it? It's like going into the nursing homes. You gc in there and you look around and you think: My God, you folks are shot. Tighten your jockstraps. Is this what awaits? It's all good. We all end up in Disneyland. You get my point."

"Actually, I don't, Skipper. That's some of the weirdest shit I've ever heard. Get the hell off the mound."

"What?"

"Get the hell off the mound. All of you. Back off. Win or lose, I'm closing."

"Now see here!"

"Back! All of you."

Squatty's leaning forward on his toes, ready to rip his throat out. He hates pitchers who won't turn over the ball.

Skipper puts his hand out. "Ball."

"No. It's my mound. It's my ball."

"I'm warning you."

"Fuck off."

Skipper's eyebrows twitch. He looks suddenly old and tired and beaten.

"Well, then," Skipper says. "Well, then. If that's the way you want it. There's nothing more to say." He hitches his trousers. He gives Smitty a long, sad look. He sighs and makes his belly-jutting trot back to the dugout.

Squatty pulls down his face guard. "I hope you're happy now. You hurt the old man's feelings."

The drooling batter awaits. The bat reaches up to the sky, a towering tree in his hands, and he makes practice swings that send currents of air back at Smitty. His legs tremble. Squatty's flashing his fingers again—who knows what pitch he's calling—and Skipper stands outside the dugout, his outstretched hands lifted to the sky, as if praying for rain.

He arcs back and he's going to throw the one no wants him to. Squatty senses it, Skipper knows, and they're shouting, *No!* But here it comes, the knuckler, floating out heavy, slow, corkscrewing, up, down, and where it goes nobody knows.

Except the batter. He shoots a liner right back at his head. The comet's streaking for his head, a white flash of light, and he drops.

The earth spins beneath him. He falls through a rip in time and space and—

He's fourteen again and he's back in the hallway of his house with his father holding the electric clippers, telling him it's time to come down to the utility room for his haircut. But this time Smitty is explaining in a polite, reasonable way that he doesn't want to be defiant but it just makes him feel humiliated to walk into school with a buzzed head, and this time the old man takes it in calmly and says, You know, you're right, Smitty. I see your point. What if I just give you a light trim around the ears and we call it good? Yeah, Smitty says. Yeah, I can live with that. And they shake hands and they're buddies again.

He opens his eyes and they're standing over him, looking down anxiously. Skipper, Squatty, the infielders.

"Sorry, Skipper. I shouldn't have thrown the knuckler."

Skipper chuckles. "No, it's okay, Smitty. It worked out fine. The ball bounced off your head and rolled to Shortie and we turned a double play. We thought of calling an ambulance for you, but you know the cost of that. I'd have to get authorization."

"We won?"

"We sure did. Guess you can keep closing for us."

"I'm going to the Majors. The Show!"

Squatty snorts.

"Forget it, kid," Skipper says. "You're washed up. No offense."

But that's okay. He closes his eyes and he's in Iowa once more—hot, muggy afternoon—and he's lighting up the electronic timer. Ninety miles per hour, ninety-five, one hundred, *one hundred and five!*

That's a fantastic fast ball, kid! You got any other pitches?

He winds up. Oh, yeah, I got lots of pitches. I got more pitches than you ever dreamed of. *Here comes one now.*

TEACH US

SHOW US SOME THINGS, we ask our new teacher. We sit in the floor in a circle, looking at him as he stands surrounded by us.

We are young, though not children. He is older, but not old, though a look crosses his face as if he is tired, as if he has seen things he wishes he had not seen.

He doesn't really want to teach us. His eyes slide to the metal door as if he's measuring the steps, calculating how quickly he can escape.

I don't know that I really have anything to show you, he says.

But we heard that you were good. You won tournaments.

To tell the truth, he says, that was mostly a myth. I had a good day now and then. Once or twice I was lucky. But that was a long time ago.

Why have you come here then?

For the money, he says, though it's not much. But I suppose I can't expect better at this point.

Still, we say, you're here. Show us something. Show us the one-finger push.

The one-finger push, he says. Yes, well, it would probably work on most of you. You're not so tough looking. But what about him? The big fellow?

The big fellow grins and rises to his feet. His biceps bulge from his T-shirt. Beneath his gray shorts his huge calf muscles twitch. He played linebacker in college. He has the shifty eyes of one accustomed to being attacked from several directions at once. He grins. Sure, push me.

The teacher sighs. He is not large. There's a bit too much pot to his belly. You are very strong, he says. I don't know if this will work on you.

Come on, the big fellow, the linebacker, says.

The teacher touches his index finger to the center of the linebacker's chest. The linebacker grins, but the lines tighten around his eyes.

The teacher gives a small, almost imperceptible push with his finger. The linebacker goes nowhere. If anything, his feet sink deeper into the floor. Hah! he snorts. He swells up with blood and muscle. He looks like he could charge and drive the teacher into the wall, shatter his spine and the back of his head. It looks hopeless for the teacher. We feel badly for him, but we are angry too. Why did he come here when we are already in such despair? What does he know of our troubles? He may feel trapped like us, but at the end of the day he will be free to leave.

The teacher frowns. You're even bigger than I thought, he says.

Come on, the linebacker says. Take another shot.

He frowns. He shrugs his shoulders. He pushes again and the linebacker steps back.

The teacher's shoulders sink pleasurably as if he's just been massaged. Step in here again, he says to the linebacker.

He steps back in and again the teacher springs him back with a little push of his finger. The big fellow stops grinning; he grimaces, his face turns red. Time and again the teacher lightly pushes and makes him step back.

Sweat pours down the linebacker's face. The veins beat in his temples. The cords stand out on his thick neck. He sinks into a ballplayer's stance, one fist apelike on the ground, the other arm across his massive thigh. His calf muscles throb. He crouches on his toes, ready to burst through the line and sack the quarterback. The teacher makes a small sound in his throat—it might be a chuckle—and he touches the side of the linebacker's shoulder and thrusts him to the floor.

The linebacker bounces up grinning. He tries to pull grass from his teeth, though there is no grass in this windowless room. The linebacker's eyes travel into the past, into packed, cheering stadiums. He travels into bright, chilly afternoons, his jersey stained with blood, his breath panting in puffs of fog between the bars of his face guard. Travels into bright, chilly afternoons, the scent of smoke and dying autumn in the air.

Hah! he snaps. This guy's great!

But already the teacher's shoulders are drawing in, and the light fades from his eyes. He shrugs.

Can you teach us that?

No.

Why not?

I don't know how to teach it. I could line you up and demonstrate it again and again and we would get nowhere. I could have you practice it repeatedly and it would not work. You all seem a little slow to me. I'm not complaining. If I were you, I would go to another teacher, if possible. There are young people who know how to explain it. It seems mostly a matter of luck to me. Sometimes I'm lucky. I could be humiliated a minute from now. You could push me right over.

Could we try? we ask.

He sighs. All right, then. If you must.

One by one we charge in on him. Sometimes he stands there like an oak, letting us push on him until we fall exhausted to the floor. Other times he turns his waist like a matador and we go stumbling past him. Finally, we all wade in on him at once and he spins about, his arms moving like great windmills, and he whirls us into the corners and walls.

Teach us, teach us, please, we cry eagerly. How do you do it?

Luck, he whispers, almost with hatred. I don't know. He stares fiercely at us. Let me be.

We sink back down on the floor in our circle, lost in our despair. The linebacker's eyes glaze over. He is running off the field with the cheerleaders jumping on the sideline. Their skirts flip up on their magnificent legs. They cheer, Big fellow! Big fellow! Big fellow! as they wave their pompoms. The linebacker sits with us now, both knees all zippered with stitches.

I'll be here once a week, the teacher says. That's all I can do.

We look up at him. Our eyes widen. You'll teach us?

I'll be here.

You'll show us the one-finger push?

I'll be here, he says.

We look at each other. Something loosens and opens in our chests. The linebacker slaps his palms on his great thighs. Whoo-hoo! he chortles. Here we go!

The teacher turns. Next week, he calls over his shoulder. He leaves us there as the guard lets him out. We sit, shoulders bumping together, a clock ticking in the silence.

EPISODE

MY OLDER BROTHER, LEN, is off his meds again. I've felt his breakdown coming the last couple of days, though my father hasn't wanted to face up to it yet. This morning Len came into my bedroom and looked at one of my paintings on the wall, something I'd done in art school, an abstract southwestern landscape sort of thing, and not all that great. He stared at it, riveted, his eyes tearing up. "That's the most beautiful painting I've ever seen," he said. "That should be in the Dallas Museum of Art. That should be in the Louvre." With his strong arms he drew me to his chest. "I can *feel* that horse between my thighs. That's me with the lance in my hands." He moved closer to the painting, eyes round and shiny. "No, I'm both. I'm the Comanche *and* the one being chased. God, that's brilliant! You're a *genius!*" I stared at my painting, but hard as I tried I could not see a single Comanche. At least I had not consciously included an Indian in the painting. There was only the prairie rolling away to the distance, and some trees and boulders and lots of colorful swirls. He released me from his embrace, then gripped both my hands and held them in his calloused palms. "Don't do manual labor with these," he said. "Don't be like me. I'll send you money when you need it."

He disappeared for the day, and now he's surfaced late at night, and we sit at the kitchen table as he sips whiskey, a vain attempt to calm himself. Every few seconds his hand opens and shuts like a man giving blood. Len's thirty-two and I'm twenty-five, but since he started having his bipolar disorder a few years ago I feel like the older brother. He moved back home with my father a few months ago, and I'm back home this summer after grad school, trying to get my bearings and move on.

He squints his eyes, cocks an ear, listening for something, listening maybe for the sounds of the horses' hooves, the horses carrying the Comanche back through time into a moonlight raid on our house in the hilly suburbs north of Austin. Len has a thing about the Comanche; even when we were kids, in a kind of love and hate he'd talk in awe of them as the greatest horse warriors who ever lived. He's been staying up all night this week reading Larry McMurtry's *Lonesome Dove* trilogy, James Michener's *Texas*, and my mother's roots material about our family's frontier days, devouring hundreds of pages of the novels and the family lore, apparently not the best reading material if you're manic.

I take a breath, trying to steady my voice when I speak. "Listen, Len. I talked to Dr. Wilson."

He lurches back as if stabbed, eyes widening at the mention of Dr. Wilson, the psychiatrist who's seen off and on for the last few years. "That old hack?" he says. "Doctor Electrode? You got anybody else on the list? I mean, Kenneth, *really* . . ." He leans in close, breathing his whisky breath in my face, eyes turning squinty and wizened, like a con man working a deal. "Do we have any back up? Do we have a fucking plan here or not?"

"I should drive you down to the hospital, Len. You know, just get checked out."

His voice edges into bitterness. "You mean checked *in*? Whose side are you on, Kenneth? Whose side?"

I feel my throat tightening. "I'm on your side, Len. You know that."

He takes another swig at his whiskey glass. "Hey, I'm feeling good. I can handle this. This will all be gone in the morning. We'll play golf. Do you want to play golf in the morning? Because I plan to play golf in the morning, and I'd like you to come." He smiles widely. "It'll be great, playing golf with you again." He cackles with sudden laughter. "I'm not carrying your bag anymore! Remember the way you used to make me carry your bag when you got tired? You're old enough to carry your own damn bag this time!"

I sit there, not answering, until he demands, "So do you want to play golf or not?"

I shrug my shoulders. "Sure, Len, whatever."

He lets out a long breath between tight lips and leans in, eyes anxious. "Seriously, do I seem a little weird or something?"

"Oh, no, not at all. You don't seem weird at all, Len."

His shoulders shake with quiet laughter as he gets the sarcasm, knowing I think he's being weird as hell, but the opening allows me to tell him the truth. "Len, I think you're having an episode. We've got to get some help."

He lowers his head, contemplates the suggestion for a moment, considers the weeks ahead in the hospital, the medications, and he sits back, squaring his shoulders as if to ward off something coming at him too fast and hard. "It happened here," he says in a hushed voice. "Right here. Close your eyes. Listen."

I stare at him until he hisses, *"Close your eyes."*

I close my eyes, and I hear a faint wind against the windows. I hear his breathing, a heavy, agitated sound. I hear the tinkle of ice in his glass. *"Do you hear it?"* he asks.

I keep my eyes closed. "Hear what, Len? Hear what?"

"The screaming."

I open my eyes. His lips tremble with excitement. "Do you get it now?" he asks. "It happened here—right here. Mother knew. She hinted at it. She was going to break it to me first. She knew I was the only one who could handle it."

"What are you talking about?"

"Her roots stuff she was always looking into. Great-Great Uncle Ira, the one who fought the Comanche?"

"I don't remember anything about it."

"God, how could I have missed it? Can't you hear the screaming?

People *died* here. That's what she was trying to tell me. The house is full of spirits. It always *has* been."

I shake my head. "I just hear the wind, Len. It's just the wind."

He smiles, nods his head with the pretend patience of one dealing with a slow-learning child. "Remember the arrowheads we found when we were kids?"

"Mom said those were from a peaceful tribe."

"Of *course* she would tell you that. She tried to protect you." He leans in close, eyes gouging into mine, his voice a rapid, hoarse whisper. "She *knew*. She referred to a ranch not far from here. A ranch where Uncle Ira lived with his wife and son. But it was *here*. Our house is built right over the bloody soil. *This* is where they fought and died."

"In the *kitchen*?" I rock back in my chair, creating a little more space between us. "Holy shit, Len. You're freaking the hell out of me."

He stares at me, eyes glittering. "They killed his wife and made off with the little boy. He grew up with the Comanche, but he was ransomed back. Only he was never the same. He was wild. He could never adjust." Len's been hiding something in his lap and now he brings it up onto the table, a butcher knife from one of our kitchen drawers. "They were up in the hills watching. Then they rode in. It was pure adrenaline back then, Kenneth. Late at night, listening, wondering if this was the night they punched your ticket. It's coming clear to me now. My God, it all makes sense now."

He presses the point of the knife against the Formica table and spins it. He clasps it during its wobbly rotation. "I like knives," he says. "Do you like knives?"

"They're okay," I say, hearing the quiver in my voice. "I kind of like butter knives. Do you want me to get you a butter knife?"

"I've always liked sharp knives," he says. "The beauty, the power, the symmetry." He tests the air with the blade. Short and thick-muscled, Len's a pretty tough guy from his years of construction work and studying the martial arts. He's let his hair get shaggy and his ragged beard has some streaks of blood or ketchup in it. He stands and swoops around the kitchen, doing deep knee bends, coming up, sweeping the air with the knife. "Come at me," he whispers to an imaginary enemy.

We hear a cough in the hallway, a clearing of a throat, and Len's face suddenly changes. He retreats to his chair at the kitchen table, and, as if some calming wax has been spread over his features, his wild eyes sink inward, his agitated brow seals into a smooth surface, and with a quick motion he hides the knife beneath his shirt.

"You boys are up late," my father says, wandering in his old bathrobe into the kitchen, going to the sink for a glass of water. Maybe my father's seen the knife, but he doesn't let on. I think he tells himself he hasn't seen it.

Since my mother's death a year ago he wears an eternally fragile, bewildered expression. He sleeps poorly, in his tattered bathrobe moves about the house like a ghost, checking doors and windows in the night. Lately, for the first time I can remember, he seems troubled by his Korean War experiences. He never talked about the war when we were growing up, and even now he says little, but sometimes he gets a faraway look. A couple of mornings ago he stood at the sliding glass door, looking at our large, well–cared for backyard, and he said to himself, quite clearly and distinctly, continuing an interior conversation, "He's been dead all these years. He never had a chance."

I joined him at the glass door and asked him whom he was referring to. My father didn't start a family until he was older than usual, and even when we were kids he kept his distance in a detached, kindly sort of way. But he likes being asked questions, and he always responds politely, even generously.

"Bill Richards," he said. "One of my friends in Korea." He took off his glasses and rubbed at his tired eyes. "Not my best friend. But a good friend. A sweet guy. Not a mean bone in his body. Nineteen when he got killed. I woke up thinking about him. I've been alive all this time and he never had a chance. He was just getting started." He made a kind of waving gesture out at the backyard, as if to indicate all the things in life that Bill Richards never got to experience.

He put his glasses back on. "When did that get so dirty?" he asked. His eyes had focused on the birdbath near the patio. "When did the birds decide to poop all over that?"

My father's become more philosophical and introspective since my mother died. He goes to daily Mass, and I go with him some-times. He likes the 6:30 a.m., dawn special. The priest doesn't fart around at that hour; he gets the crew in and out in thirty minutes. Everybody there beside me is old, and they look beat up. With stiff hips they hobble up for communion. But I admire them. They endure. They go on.

My father sits down with us at the kitchen table, pulling up a chair between Len and me. "What were you talking about?"

Len pinches his lips shut. He clams up around my father. Afraid he'll give away his secret. That he's losing it again. My father's always the one who ends up signing the hospital papers.

"We were talking about the frontier days," I tell my father. "The Comanche."

"Oh," my father says. "That sure was a long time ago. Do you boys remember when this house was first built, all the mud instead of grass?"

"It wasn't so long ago, Dad," Len says with a quaver in his voice. "It wasn't so long ago. Do we have to pretend it never happened? Do we have to ignore the dead Indian on the table?"

My father blinks and squints at the table as if looking for the dead Indian. Len's hand reaches out to clutch my father's robe near his throat. My father's pale, skinny chest seems to pulse. Len stares in wonder at the robe, running the fabric between his fingers. "That's the most beautiful robe I've ever seen, Dad."

My father chuckles. "This old thing?" But he sounds pleased by the compliment.

Len's eyes mist over. "You're a beautiful man, Dad. You break my heart. You're Saint Francis of Assisi. I just want to take you in my arms and hold you."

My father draws his robe tighter about him, easing away from Len. "Say, let's have some pie," he says. "As long as we're up."

"That's a great idea, Dad." I follow him to the refrigerator. "Dad," I whisper, "I told you so. Len's having an episode."

My father leans in and out of the fridge and hands me an aluminum dish with congealed peach pie in it. "Should we have some ice cream too? Do you want to get some bowls, Kenneth?"

As my father ladles ice cream over the wedges of pie, Len's poised at the table. Listening. Watching us. Prepared to bolt.

We bring the bowls back to the table and my father sits between Len and me. "Didn't your mother have something about the Comanche in her roots stuff?" my father asks. "She used to love that old stuff, but I could never get very worked up about it. I wish I'd paid more attention to it now, for her sake."

"You're damn right she had stuff about the Comanche," Len says, his voice cracking with righteous indignation. "You're damn right she did! They came howling out of the hills, dragged Uncle Ira into the night, cut off his balls, and staked him out on the plains."

My father swallows a big lump of pie. "My God," he says. "I never knew that."

"You had to read between the lines. They killed his wife and made off with his son. Uncle Ira survived. But he went crazy. He rode after them, became a vigilante. He did terrible things. Burned their villages. Killed women and children. He became a horror even to himself."

My father stares into space, holding his spoon in midair. Then he says, a little sadly, "Well, it was all a long time ago, Len."

"By the time they found the boy nobody recognized him. Even his own father, Uncle Ira. The boy didn't know where he belonged anymore. He had a raccoon for a pet, but it got rabies and died. Uncle Ira disappeared in the Gold Rush. The boy became an outlaw, then a sheriff, or he was a sheriff and then an outlaw. Mother wasn't clear about that. She always wanted a happy ending. Finally, he just disappeared too. You could read between the lines."

We look at Len and we realize there are tears splashed on his cheeks. My father touches Len's hand. "You miss your mother. I've been missing her too. All that roots stuff. It makes you think of her."

Len springs back from his touch, smashes his fist down on the table. "Are you both out of your minds?" he screams. "Don't you understand anything I've been trying to tell you? Stop pretending you don't know what happened here!"

"My God, Len. Easy, son," my father says. He reaches out to embrace Len, but Len shouts, "I will not abide it! This is an outrage! An outrage!"

He pushes my father away and ducks out the sliding glass door into the backyard. We follow him into the thick heat of a full moon's summer night. My father raises his hand to his mouth and bites at the flesh between his thumb and index finger. "Oh, God, not again," he mutters. "Not again." He puts out his hand, tries to catch up with Len, who has retreated toward the flowerbed at the far side of the lawn.

"Watch it, Dad. Len's got a knife."

"He wouldn't hurt us. He doesn't have a mean bone in his body."

"We've got to get him to the hospital, Dad, before something happens."

"Len?" my father shouts across the lawn. "*Len?*" His voice sounds like something cracking in two.

Len strides back and forth on the far side of the lawn, near the flowerbed. We cross the yard, huge shadows floating before us.

"Wow!" he says happily. "Fireflies!" He grabs our shoulders like a school kid with his buddies. "Look at all the fireflies, you guys! Don't you love fireflies? God, I love fireflies!"

My father and I look around as Len points. "There! Over there! Do you remember putting them in jars, Kenneth? Putting them in jars in a dark room and they glowed?" He punches my arm. "But you always made me let them go. You were so smart. You were so sensitive. God, I adore you. You're the best person I know. You are too, Dad. You're the best person I know. There's something sexy about you. I don't mean that in any weird sort of way."

My father rubs the side of his face, as if wondering if he's missed a shave. "I don't know why we don't have fireflies like we used to," he says. "We used to have fireflies all over the place, and we'd come out here, all of us, and your mother . . ."

Len chuckles as if listening to a child. "Don't be silly, Dad. We *still* have fireflies. Look at them! They're everywhere!"

My father and I stand in the hot, humid air; the yard looks much the same as always, the expanse of neat lawn, the flowerbed, the oak trees with their huge branches, the shrubs back by the alley, and the only thing amiss with the picture is that there aren't any fireflies. Not a one. If I were to paint the scene, I would have to imagine the fireflies.

"Don't you see them? Don't you *see* them?" He steps between us and looks desperately at us, as if we're playing a trick on him. "Are you guys *blind*?"

"Len," my father says heavily. He frowns down at his feet, his next words seeming to leak out of his mouth one by one. "We've got to do something about this, son."

Len recoils from us, making a cross with his fingers as if warding off a vampire. His shadow lengthens. As he whirls around to run, he stumbles and it gives me time to catch him. I try to tackle him, but he's twice as strong. He sends me flying. My father takes hold of his arm, but Len throws him to the ground. He pins my father's chest with his tennis-shoed foot. The knife comes out from underneath his shirt and he bends and holds it to my father's throat. "Don't make me kill you," he says. "Just ride off."

I ease myself toward them, afraid to come too fast. Afraid to startle him. I find my voice cracking. "Please, Len. It's Dad. It's Dad, Len."

He looks up at me, as if through a mesh screen, in the full

moonlight blinking to get me in focus. His eyes fill with tears and he shudders and drops the knife, and I move in quickly to take it away and throw it up on the patio. He embraces my father, wedging his hands under my father's armpits and pulling him into a sitting position. "I'm sorry, Daddy. I'm sorry. Help me, Daddy. God, help me."

"I will, son. I will." He cradles Len's head. "My sweet boy . . ."

"I can work through this, Daddy. Everything will be fine. You'll see. I'm playing golf in the morning. Just like old times. Like normal."

My father shakes his head, his voice coming cut in a moan. "It's not normal, Len. Nothing's normal right now."

Len grips my father's arms, his blunt fingers digging into the flesh, his eyes wide and frightened. "I won't make it home this time, Daddy." He hangs his head. "Don't leave me there. Don't forget me."

My father's voice grows stronger. "We'll never forget you, Len. We'll make it home. I promise."

"I won't go back." He shoves my father away, and my father rocks back in the blue, shadowed grass, thin, pale legs beneath his bathrobe swinging up in the air like a rising seesaw.

I dive at Len, but he breaks for it. At the far side of the lawn he springs nimbly over the chain-link fence into Mr. Robinson's backyard. My father sits up with a start, as if an alarm clock has blared in his ear. "The Doberman!" he cries.

Mr. Robinson's automatic floodlights click on and illuminate his yard. I help my father up and we hurry after Len to the fence, in time to see the Doberman, old Jeeter, eighteen now, go into his hound of the Baskervilles act. With the guttural snarl of an enraged drillmaster, he staggers stiff-legged across his turf. He's a horrid looking thing, one-eyed, with scabby patches of orange-tinted, medicated fur. The old dinosaur moves on memory. One last glorious mission. One last neighborhood ass to chew.

As old Jeeter bares his teeth and hunches his shoulders to leap at Len, Len gives an ear-splitting karate cry, reminiscent of a man being skewered alive, and launches a sidekick at Jeeter's head. He misses, but Jeeter yelps in fear. Tangling his legs in the retreat, Jeeter rolls like a flipped wrestler, but rage gives him youth and he springs back at Len, who yells, "Yow!" and breaks for the trampoline. He jumps up on it, and Jeeter yaps proudly as Mr. Robinson, in his bathrobe, perennial drink in hand, comes out on the flagstone patio. He observes Len bounce up and down on the trampoline, and he gives my father and me a friendly wave.

"Hoo, boy," Mr. Robinson says with a chuckle. "Calm down, Jeeter, you old asshole. Don't give yourself a stroke."

Jeeter stops yapping, but he patrols the perimeter of the trampoline while Len bounds up and down, going higher and higher. "Hi, there, Mr. Robinson," Len calls from midair.

"Howdy, Len. You know, I don't know if that old tramp will hold you anymore. Mostly just the grandkids use it now." He pauses, cracks ice between his teeth. "Little guys."

Len tucks, lands on his butt, bounces back to his feet. "Feels okay."

Mr. Robinson chuckles. He's got a way of cracking ice in his teeth and talking at the same time. "Glad to know it's held up. It just sits out in the rain. I think the kids oil the springs sometimes when they're in town."

"Hey, there, John," my father calls. We lean over the chain-link fence and wave at Mr. Robinson.

"Hey, there, Tom, Kenneth." While Jeeter stands guard over Len, Mr. Robinson joins us at the fence. His bathrobe, a thick, creamy beige, is in much better shape than my father's. He's a bullish looking man of seventy-eight, with thick, white calves beneath the robe.

My father clears his throat. "I'm mighty sorry to disturb you, John. We've got a kind of situation going on with Len again."

Mr. Robinson swings his head around to study Len bouncing high on the tramp, legs spread-eagle at the top of his flight. "I suspected that, Tom. Well, Len's welcome to bounce all night, if it helps. Anything I can do?"

My father sighs. "Thank you, John. We're mighty obliged. He'll calm down and then we'll drive him to the hospital. He'll be ready to go."

"Come on over. Old Jeeter won't bite you. This has really sparked him up. He hasn't chased one of your boys in years."

I start to climb the fence and Mr. Robinson chuckles and cracks ice in his teeth. "You can use the gate now, Ken."

We go out our side gate and through Mr. Robinson's into his yard and we shake hands. His big hand engulfs mine and I feel my knuckles pop when he squeezes.

"How's Annie, John?" my father asks.

Mr. Robinson gets a tight sound in his throat. "Not so good, Tom. Not so good."

"I'm sorry to hear that."

He shrugs, the collar of his bathrobe shifting a little around his broad neck. "You know the score, Tom. You fellas want a drink?"

"No, thanks, John. We'll just wait here."

"I'm going to check on Annie. She's restless tonight."

Mr. Robinson goes inside to check on his wife. I eye old Jeeter, but he looks nervous to be left alone with us. He retreats to the patio and hides under the swinging bench.

"Look at this!" Len calls. He bounces high and turns a flip, landing neatly on his feet.

"My God, Len. Don't do that," my father says. "Do you want to hurt yourself?"

"I'm good," Len says. "Aren't I good?"

"Sure. But you don't need to prove anything."

"Drumroll, please." He launches another flip. He stumbles as he lands, running forward a couple of steps, but stopping before he falls. "Ta-dah!" He holds his arms aloft, the Olympic winner on display.

Mr. Robinson appears with a fresh drink. "Len, you're going to give my insurance agent a fit."

Len talks to my father as he bounces. "How come you didn't give me gymnastics lessons when I was a kid? I could have amounted to something."

"I didn't know you wanted gymnastics classes."

"I did, but I just didn't know it back then."

"Would you like to come down and have a scotch, Len?" Mr. Robinson asks. "Or maybe some milk? Buttermilk? Maybe we got some old buttermilk around here, in a jar someplace. I fancy a nice cold drink of buttermilk now and then myself . . ." He frowns at his glass, jostles the liquid around a little and murmurs, "Though this works in a pinch."

"I could have been a Flying Wallenda!" The springs creak in the old trampoline as Len flies higher and higher. He pulls his knees up, tucks his head to flip.

"No, Len!" my father cries.

He doesn't get all the way around, but crashes on his neck and shoulder. He lets out a moan and curls into a ball.

"Len!" Dad shouts. "Are you hurt, son?"

"Aw, hell, Tom, you're going to clean me out," Mr. Robinson says with profound resignation. "I'll call my insurance agent. There goes the boat." He sighs, shakes the ice in his glass around. "Shit. I wanted to leave something to the kids."

I jump on the trampoline to help Len, but he rolls over the springs to the ground. Clutching his neck like a man waking up with a terrific charley horse, he lurches over the lawn, falls into the swimming pool, and sinks straight to the bottom.

I do a moonwalk to the other side of the tramp and jump hard to the ground, falling and skinning my knees. As I pull my T-shirt over my head, my father pinches my arms with skinny, strong fingers. "Don't! He'll drag you down!" He kneels on the edge of the pool and puts his face near the water and shouts, "Get up here right now, Len! I mean it!"

"I've got a long pole here someplace," Mr. Robinson says. "A cleaning net. I think I can hook him."

I jump in, feet first. When I sink down to the bottom, I see Len doing a kind of underwater ballet act. In a bluish light he pirouettes, spreads his arms, operatic, Romeo beckoning to Juliet. His hair's blown back in the water. When he sees me his eyes widen as if a fearsome creature has swum into God's glorious lagoon. He slugs me in the jaw and leaps on me. A long pole pokes into the back of my neck and a net wraps around my face. Len gets me in a headlock and kicks us toward the surface. He's seventeen again. A lifeguard once more. The best in the neighborhood. The best everything.

He drags me out and throws me on the tiles bordering the pool. He frees my face from the cleaning net, begins to administer CPR, but then jumps back in horror. His finger traces the long scar on my chest from my heart surgery when I was a child.

"They cut his heart out!" he shrieks.

As Len runs for the street side of the corner lot, Jeeter streaks out from under the swinging bench like a torpedo released from its chute. Len's a step ahead as he hits the fence. He leaps to hurdle it and howls as he lands. He's caught on the fence, straddling it, while Jeeter gnaws at his jeans. Len topples free and limps into the night, running beneath the full moon, a crazed scout turned loose on the neighborhood.

Mr. Robinson holds his cleaning net like a lance. "Well, this has been a hell of a night," he says.

He leads us to the gate. Old Jeeter struts behind. He growls low in his throat, gives me a last malevolent glare. Next time, punk, he warns. Next time.

Mr. Robinson shakes my father's hand. "Good luck, Tom. Come back for a drink sometime. Don't be a stranger, Ken."

An apparition appears on the lawn. A woman all in white, aglow in the moonlight.

"Are the boys home?" a trembling voice calls. "Is it the boys?" She opens her arms to us, her white nightgown full of billowy loose folds.

"Oh, hell," Mr. Robinson mutters. "Go inside, Annie," he calls. "Go inside." He gives me a sudden, forceful hug, drawing me into a thick neck scented with aftershave. "Go find him, Kenneth. *Find him!*"

He turns to comfort his wife. She's on her knees, sobbing near the trampoline, and he lifts her gently under the arms and leads her inside.

We back my father's sedan out of the garage. I drive in my wet clothes, and my father pulls his bathrobe tighter about his throat.

We prowl the neighborhood. It's a nicely established neighborhood now, new when I was growing up, a mix of ranch and two-story brick houses. One house up the block has white columns in front, but it has always stood out as pretentious.

We catch glimpses of Len hiding behind trees, darting down alleyways. Our headlights zoom in on him as he crouches behind some trash cans. He shields his eyes with his arm, then runs.

He crosses Bandera Road into a rough part of town. Shotgun homes. Peeling paint. Broken machinery in the yards. The oaks and willows press hard to the road, branches untrimmed, and our lights sweep into the shrubbery alongside the houses, probe into the secret places.

A new brick apartment building has gone up. It has a gentrified look, an attempt to reclaim this part of town. A keg party's underway on the balustrade and revelers spill in and out of open doorways.

My father adjusts the flaps of his robe over his thighs. "When did this all happen?" he asks. "When did it all happen?"

Our headlights catch up with Len as he races across a weedy, vacant lot. Deer-like, he freezes a moment before sprinting off again, and for a moment I feel like I enter his world. One oak ahead in the distance. A lone runner on the prairie, arms raised to take an arrow in the back, the hooves of the horses pounding after him.

A MORNING SWIM

JILL WAS STILL SLEEPING so he got out of bed quietly, and in the bathroom he pulled on his swimming suit and stepped into his sandals. She was still sleeping when he left the rental cottage that overlooked the bay. He planned to be back from his swim before she even woke because he knew she would worry. Earlier in the summer there had been stories in the local paper about shark sightings all up and down the Cape, even close to shore, but there hadn't been any reports in almost a month now, and at any rate, not a single soul in the area had been attacked and what were the odds anyway? He wasn't an overly cautious person, but he was hardly reckless.

The cottage was on a bluff and he walked down a long, sandy boardwalk to a narrow beach, crossed the beach, and went out on a short pier. Sometimes there were people out fishing, but it was just after dawn now and he was the only one out. He left his T-shirt and his sandals at the end of the pier. There was a ladder to ease himself into the water, which was cold year-round but quite swimmable now in late July. The first touch of the water was the most difficult and his legs pimpled and tightened against it. He took a breath and sank into the water. A shock traveled through his chest, but after submerging and coming back up, the chill eased and he looked ahead to the orange and white buoy about a hundred yards away. He'd made the swim daily earlier in the summer when they'd first arrived, before the shark sightings induced Jill to make him stop for a time. But he was ready to take it on again. He wasn't a great swimmer, but certainly decent. He regularly swam a mile at the swimming pool back home and at amateur competitions even placed reasonably well in the over fifty-five age division. Open water swimming was quite different from pool swimming, but a hundred yards out then back was easy. Usually he'd do some repeats, catching his breath in between by hanging on the ladder.

He started slowly, with casual breast strokes. The water was calm and now that he'd adjusted to the cold he felt quite peaceful. He enjoyed the solitude, having a little time to his own. He and Jill rarely fought, but sometimes there was an irritability and distance between them, which seemed more pronounced of late. They weren't used to spending so much time together. He'd taken an early retirement and she was still going strong in her law practice, but she'd agreed to take an extended vacation. In the first couple of weeks they'd enjoyed themselves. Each day they'd bike the two miles to the town center to sit in a café and talk and then bring home a few groceries in their knapsacks. But the novelty had worn off and now they usually just drove and parked at the supermarket.

After fifty yards he switched to a slow crawl, then a bit faster, but steady, controlled. He'd take it easy on the way out and then sprint it back home. At first it always seemed as if the orange and white buoy was coming no closer, but now he bobbed up in the water long enough to get a clearer view and the buoy loomed just up ahead. There was something comforting in its nearness. That's when he felt the sensation, the water move below him, a rushing of water past his thighs, and whirling his head about he saw nothing for a few seconds until ten yards to his right a fin jutted from the water and glided on. The fin turned in a circle and disappeared below the water.

He dashed for the buoy, wrapping his arms and legs around it, attempted to climb it, but the buoy tottered down toward him so as he tried to climb it, it came down with him and pushed him back into the water. He raked at it, sought a hold, but it kept bobbing and throwing him off. It seemed to be mocking him, to be his enemy. He remembered reading that sharks were attracted by motion, by indications of distress. With his legs he pushed back from the buoy. He moved his arms and legs slowly, side stroking toward shore with delicate movements of his arms and legs. Easy. No sudden motions.

Halfway home he abandoned all effort at calm and dug for the shore, legs kicking hard. He felt the water swell beneath him. The pier was off to his right so he went straight for the beach until his feet found sand. He ran out of the water, glanced back as if fearing the creature would follow him up on shore. He saw nothing in the water. He fell to his knees in the sand, gasped for air, then sprawled flat out on the beach. He lay in the sand, chest throbbing until it was difficult to tell whether it was his own heart he was feeling or whether the sand was pulsing up through him with a beat that slowed and grew steadier, as if he were taking in moment by moment the pleasure and strength of the earth. He was covered in sand. His chest, his face. He didn't care. The sand felt exquisite. He rolled over. He looked up at the sky. My God, it was beautiful. He laughed, thinking what a cliché he was. That's what everybody said—have a near death experience, if that's what it was, and everything was suddenly beautiful.

Before retirement, for many years he had taught writing at a community college. His students had always been writing about how they'd had a scary experience, but it had taught them to "live life to the fullest." He'd always groaned when he read that, but now, wow, that was exactly it—he didn't quite know what it all entailed, but he wanted to live life to the fullest! It was ridiculous. He knew he was reading way too much into this, but he felt changed, more alive than he had in years. Vibrant! That was the word. He felt vibrant. And blessed! Yes, that too!

He stood up. He scanned the water with his eyes. No fins anywhere in sight. Could it have been a dolphin? Or a more benevolent sort of shark? But he saw the fin in his mind now, how ominous it had looked. Not warm—not like a dolphin at all. But beautiful too, in its sinister, silent passing. He felt he must tell someone, issue some sort of alert, but there was still no one on the beach. After all, it wasn't exactly an alert he wanted to issue. More a sharing. He wanted to share the way he and the shark had been alone in the water, just the two of them—man, creature—and how close he'd felt to death. He'd describe how he'd kept his wits as he swam away from the buoy, though he might not emphasize the way he'd tried to climb up it. He didn't bother retrieving his shirt or sandals from the pier. He must hurry and share the story with Jill. After all, she was the one he always wanted to share with. Maybe that was the one you really loved, the one you wanted to share your stories with.

Barefooted, his face and chest coated in sand, he trotted up the boardwalk, meaning to burst through the cottage door and share the news with Jill, but on the boardwalk he slowed unexpectedly, because here, too, he was overcome with a great sense of beauty and wonder. How cool and firm the wood felt on his feet. He didn't mind if a sliver splintered off and pierced his skin. He would welcome the sudden purity of the pain. All was good. The sun still shining, the cries of the seagulls so lovely, so very lovely. The sound of a motorboat out on the bay. He would take Jill into his arms. He would love her as he had not loved her in years. Oh, he had loved her, but, you know, after thirty years together, maybe they needed a reawakening. The children were grown, on their own. They got together when they could, but it wasn't the same, of course. Retirement had not brought him the happiness he thought it might. But he saw now that the best days of their lives were not behind them but ahead. A family trip, that's what—all of them together again. Maybe rent a camper? Who knows? All was possible. He was glowing with life.

Usually he called out when he came in so as not to startle her, but as he came through the door of the cottage into the kitchen he was silent. He hadn't planned to enter silently, but a sudden profound sort of silence fell over his head and shoulders, bent him over a little with the weight of the silence. He didn't exactly know how to tell her, how to even begin. How to get the experience across, all that it had meant to him, the way he'd felt the beauty of the sun and sand as he came out of the water, the precious sense of being fully alive. What if she laughed and said something ironic like, "Maybe it was just a dolphin"? He would not appreciate that sort of response right now. She had to understand just what he felt—oh, maybe not immediately. Yes, maybe it would be best to start slow, to let her absorb his change over the next days and weeks until one day she looked him in the eyes and said, "You know, you changed that day in the water." And he might smile and cover her hand and say simply, as if she finally comprehended what had been so clear to him, "Yes, I did. I did change that day in the water."

And so he came in quietly, passing down a short hallway to the door of their bedroom. Light, the most glorious light, beamed through the bedroom window and fell on her as she sat on the edge of the bed in her white bathrobe, her back to him, looking so lovely, so tender, so human, not at all like a shark, her back to him, as she said into the phone with a girlish, flirting sort of laugh, "It's been two weeks. I need to feel your hands on me again. You have the most wonderful hands."

He backed out of the bedroom. To the left of the kitchen, on the ocean side, there was a sunny room with wide glass windows and cloth deck chairs. He sat there. He placed his hands on the arms of the deck chair and breathed. The arms of the chair were magnificent, cool and wonderful to the touch. He was still quite okay. Whatever force he'd gained was still with him and he could accept all. When they were younger he had suspected once or twice that she might be having an affair. But those suspicions had passed over time, and now that they'd been married for over thirty years he really hadn't expected this at all. But he was breathing with it, allowing this sudden knowledge of her infidelity to pass through him like a wave. Acceptance was like pushing off from the buoy, making calm, smooth movements to create no ripples.

After all, he'd had an affair once himself, long ago, with one of his colleagues at the college. A very nice woman who had probably pictured more of a future for them, but he hadn't allowed the affair to continue, and though he missed her for some time after, he was relieved when she took a job in a different state. The affair, along with the secrecy of it, the fact of not being able to share it with Jill, had always troubled him. The affair itself, certainly, but as well the secrecy involved in the cover-up had created a distance, a shadow fallen between them.

She came into the sunny room and gave a start. "I didn't hear you come in. My God, you're covered in sand."

He looked up at her, smiling with gentle understanding, filled with the new life force that pulsed through him, if not quite as strongly as it had been in those first moments after coming out of the water, still quite tangible. He felt warmth in his cheeks, a tingle in his hands, a reassuring tingle though, not at all like the time he'd had the near heart attack scare. "I heard you talking on the phone. About the hands touching you. I don't want to be jealous about it. We all need what we need. I had an affair myself once, long ago, and I always wanted to tell you about it."

Her eyes fluttered. She looked stunned. "What are you talking about? I was talking to Susan, in the village. The massage therapist. She gives the most wonderful massages." Her fluttering eyes had solidified now into a hot-eyed stare, her brow arching up. "What the hell do you mean you had an affair?"

He leaned back. Before her heated gaze his back pinned sweaty against the cloth chair. "Nothing . . . I don't know what I was talking about. I was just making up a story. I was almost attacked by a shark."

She pulled her robe tighter about her throat. "I don't know what to believe anymore. I don't know what to make of you. You've gotten so strange."

She turned. He lifted a hand toward her, rose and followed her into the hallway, but she slammed the bedroom door. He retreated into the sunny room. The deck chair, so kindly and welcoming moments ago, appeared fragile and forlorn. The feeling of change had left him, his thighs losing their muscle, flecks of sand falling off him and splattering to the bland-green linoleum floor. He must regain that feeling he had had. There was only one thing to do. He hurried back out. He ran down the boardwalk to the beach. He didn't bother with the pier but trotted across the beach. As he waded into the water he barely noticed the cold this time, and when the water reached his waist, he swam for the buoy. His strokes were choppy at first, full of anger and remorse. He realized he was thinking of his old colleague. They used to wander the corridors of the college together, talking, talking, sharing. Maybe he should not have let her go. The power was coming back to him. He would get back in touch with her. But he would still be with Jill. He would embrace both women; both would be embraced by the full, loving power that was in him now. No more secrets. He was almost disappointed when he felt no sensation across his legs, because he felt fearless now, invincible.

Nearing the buoy he paused, treaded water, glanced back to shore. A fisherman and his son had come out on the pier. He doubted that they would see him, but he waved. They did not wave back. It was okay. The buoy was just ahead. The buoy that had so betrayed him. But he didn't hold it again the buoy. He felt something like affection for the buoy now. He'd give it a friendly, gracious pat of forgiveness.

He made it just fine to the buoy. It was on the return trip that his arms and legs weakened. The current had shifted, was tugging him out to sea. He pulled against it, his breath shortening and his chest tightening. He wanted to reach out to the fisherman and his son, to call out for help, but they looked far away. He sank his head in the water, pulled as hard as he could for the beach, and when he paused for breath, treading water, he seemed no closer. He sank his head again. His arms were leaden now, but he willed himself to kick, spoke to himself until there was only one word in his head, one word smoothly timed to his breath: *kick, kick, kick.*

THE BIKE

HENDERSON HEARD THE AUTOMATIC garage door open-
ing and he came out to greet Janet. Her new job selling real estate
meant longer evenings away, and her late arrivals didn't fit in with
his vision of things—a cheery little supper, and over the meal an
exchange of work stories revealing small moments of triumph and
disappointment. But since she'd started the real estate job, by the
time she arrived home they were both tired.

This evening, though, she hopped out of her Honda, smiled
brightly at him, and moved to the back of her car, opening her
hand like a game show hostess displaying a prize, a shiny new red
mountain bike mounted on a rack. He did not pay attention to the
bike at first but to the rack, which he recognized. They'd had the
rack even before they were married, but he thought it had disappeared, that they had parted with it at a garage sale along with the
aging road bikes they'd quit riding years ago.

"Where'd you find that old thing?" he asked.

"I just dug around."

"*When?* I didn't notice you looking for anything."

She wore a flushed, grinning look and touched the front tire of
the bike. "Do you like it?"

He stopped frowning at the rack and studied the bike. "What are
you going to do with it?"

She rolled her eyes and made a swishing of air sound. "Well, if
you don't know what you do with a bike."

"No. No, I mean . . . Do you want some help?"

"I can do it."

As Janet untied the straps, she positioned her sturdy shoulders between him and the handlebars, which he wanted to ease from her. He pictured disasters, flights through the air, her pretty chin striking the pavement. "Couldn't you just ride an exercise bike at the gym?"

As she lifted the bike from the rack, she grunted for a moment and he reached a hand past her, touching the rear tire in an effort to help, but succeeding only in getting in the way, and as she swung the bike around, he backed off.

She propped the bike against the car and patted the hard black seat. "What do you think?"

"I didn't know you wanted another bike."

"I mentioned it a lot of times."

"You did?"

She opened the back door of the car and came out with a helmet in her hand. She pulled it over her head, working it over her long, full hair, which was still blonde except for some graying around her ears. She snapped the strap around her chin, wincing as the strap pinched her. "You could get a bike too, you know." Her hair streaming out from beneath the helmet gave her a Viking demeanor.

He shrugged. "You're not going to ride now? In the dark?"

She patted him on the chest. "Just once around the block."

She rolled the bike away from the car and swung one leg over the seat. In her slacks and flat shoes she moved gracefully, as if it hadn't been years since she'd ridden.

Her headlight cast a thin beam into the darkness as she rode down the steep driveway, and she hardly checked left or right as she wheeled into the street. Theirs was a quiet neighborhood of shady streets and light traffic, but it still did not feel right to have her riding off alone into the darkness. He stood in the driveway, looking after her, calling out too late for her to hear, "Be careful!"

Later, he would hear her words in his mind: *You could get a bike too.* What if he'd said, "Okay, sure, I'll get a bike"? Maybe he could have turned it all around right there. He could see them in his mind, the way it might have been—the two of them riding down a country lane, riding through a rain of autumn leaves, side by side, smiles of rapture on their faces. But he suspected that the image wasn't original, that he might have stolen it from antidepressant commercials. Sometimes, in the images, they were joined by Joshua, whom they'd lost ten years before when he was nine, drowned when he was off camping with another child's parents. Both he and the other boy had slipped from the bank into a swiftly moving river. No one had seen them fall, and Henderson would wonder later if Joshua had tried to rescue the other boy, and he supposed maybe the other parents wondered if their child had tried to rescue Joshua. When the images of Joshua on the bike came to him, he allowed them for a few moments, to relish Joshua again, to celebrate the perky, smiling boy he had been, but the images left him so shaken that he fled from them by working in the garden, shoveling and turning soil until his legs felt weak.

Why had it seemed so impossible, too late to say, "Yes, I'll get a bike. I'll ride with you"?

But if he'd said yes, would she have really been happy? Would they have ridden a few times, and then stored the bikes in a far corner of the garage, left the bikes to rust, more years gliding by until one day the bikes were back out in the driveway along with some boxes of books and old sweaters? Some kid would beam at one of the bikes and his dad would offer ten dollars, and then someone else would take the other, and later he and Janet would walk back inside from the garage sale, his hand on her elbow.

Maybe he'd done her a favor by not joining her on her rides. He would have slowed her down. There'd be roads he wouldn't want to take. He'd worry about the weather and what to wear and where would they stop to eat. Were they spending too much time out? Shouldn't he be grading papers or planning class or doing some terribly important things like preparing dinner or paying bills or checking the email or watering the lawn? Weren't there lots of important things he should be doing instead of riding on glorious country lanes with the leaves blowing around his ears?

It was never really a true image for him that they could have ridden off together into sunrises and sunsets. In truth he wanted to share the same things with her as always, their gardening, their quiet, peaceful meals, their walks in the neighborhood, the little adventures and routines that had made it possible the last ten years for him to rise each day, to shave, to dress, to go to work.

She rode every morning, getting up before the sun broke over the horizon. She rode in the evenings after work. When winter came she still rode on the sunny days, and on the snowy days she rode the exercise bike at the gym. Then in the spring she started day-long Sunday rides with a group, and then one week she broke the news that she was going on an overnighter with the group. He was stunned, floored, that she'd go away without him. She asked him to come along, but even if he could have kept up with her, the thought of sharing fellowship with strangers appalled him. The odd image that kept coming to his mind was this: He would stumble out of a tent into a foggy dawn and walk down to a creek where there would be a stocky, bare-chested, bearded man brushing his teeth. The bearded man's mouth would be full of toothpaste foam and the man would point and say something garbled and roll his eyes excitedly toward the creek and the woods beyond and Henderson would look and see nothing but vague shapes in the fog, while the foamy man pointed in excitement.

But maybe if he'd gone on the overnighter, she would have hung back with him, coaxed him along as they labored up a hill. When they pulled into camp at the end of the day, dead last in the group, the others would have gently teased them, but kindly brought him a cup of coffee and a bowl of stew. How many years had it been since he'd had a good bowl of stew?

There was a light in her eyes these days, a spring in her step. She looked trim and beautiful and foreign, as if he were watching her from a distance. As the spring days lengthened into summer he found himself alone in the evenings, working in the garden. As he sank a shovel into the soil he felt like a cartoon character, mimicking, pretending to be a fellow who knew what he was doing, but he only stayed there so that she might find him upon her return, digging away, looking useful and engaged and sure of himself.

He was teaching summer classes at the university, and after his late afternoon class he went into the library, looking for some fresh lecture materials. He'd been a popular teacher for the most part, but of late he realized his lectures must be slipping because students were constantly checking their cell phones and sending text messages. It was a huge library, full of nooks and crannies, and he found himself climbing up a narrow, winding staircase and coming to a set of classrooms he'd never known existed. He walked down a corridor and stared into the empty classrooms. They were carpeted, with high bookshelves and oil paintings on the walls. Cushioned seats were arranged around long wooden tables. He'd never been assigned to such elegant classrooms.

He walked down the hall and peeked through a windowed door. A professor with long, wispy white hair sat at the head of the table. There were only six students at the table, sitting as if entranced, no one moving or speaking. The professor's eyes were shut, his thin hands folded over a concave chest as if he'd just been pierced and was holding in his life's blood.

The professor drifted back into the depths of his chair, and the students sank deeper into their own seats. If they didn't rouse soon, they would be lost forever, trapped for all time in this hidden room in the library, cobwebs draping them and the white-haired professor.

As he descended the stairs Henderson's heart pounded, and as he crossed the campus his shirt clung sweatily to him. He shifted his heavy briefcase from hand to hand. His eyes took in the sandstone buildings and the red tile roofs. The sidewalks and the grassy malls were quiet on this summer evening, but he felt as if the few walkers on campus were staring at him, accusing him. Of what? What crime had he committed? On the sidewalk a familiar-looking, long-haired boy on a skateboard rolled toward him. So many semesters had gone by, Henderson confused the names of past students, but this face seemed to swim at him through a haze of years as he searched his memory for the particular class he'd had the boy in, the particular seat the boy had taken. The boy was moving fast, but Henderson tried to catch his eye. Perhaps the student would say something friendly. Perhaps he would stop to chat and he would tell Henderson that he had made a difference in his life. But the student kicked his skateboard quickly past. Looking after him, Henderson had a recollection of the boy now, and he was pretty sure he had failed him. The boy had gone by a weird nickname. Antler. He'd show up stoned and fall asleep at his desk.

He was pleased, somehow, to know that Antler was still haunting the campus. He felt a sudden warmth and benevolence toward Antler, and he wished to join him, to skateboard down the sidewalks with him. The last time he'd ridden a skateboard was when he'd tried out the one he'd bought Joshua for Christmas. He'd recalled doing it as a kid himself, and he put one foot on the board as Joshua looked on encouragingly. Then Henderson kicked with his other foot, scooted forward two feet until the front of the board lifted and tossed him back in the air. He'd landed hard on his back and elbow and lay on the sidewalk with Joshua staring down at him, asking, "Are you okay, Dad? Are you okay?" Henderson smiled through the pain. "I'm fine, Joshua."

As he walked on, with Antler disappearing into the distance, Henderson crossed a footbridge with a scummy pond below. He resisted an urge to fling his briefcase into the green water, to let it sink beneath the tadpoles. He willed the papers inside to burn, to turn to ash. He would leave it all behind, his colleagues, his students, the sandstone buildings, the walkways over which he had toted the briefcase for so many years. He would leave it all behind, start fresh with Janet.

His library search made him arrive home later than usual, and Janet was already heading out. In her shorts and T-shirt she looked slender and tanned and younger than her years as she rolled her bike out of the garage. She stopped as she saw him pull into the driveway.

He got out of the car, his shirt wet with sweat. She looked at him, not yet on the bike, steadying the handlebars.

He blocked her way. "I want to get a bike," he said. "I want to start riding with you."

What had he expected? A smile? An embrace? Tears came to her eyes. She was shaking her head.

She brushed past him. She mounted the bike and rode down the driveway and into the street. Henderson stood there, on a warm evening, covered with sweat, looking after her red shirt as she disappeared around a curve.

Later he would ponder it. The usual metaphors. A man waking out of a dream. A man coming to his senses after a fever. It was like those things, he supposed. But those metaphors missed something. They said it all and said nothing.

He followed her in his mind as she rode through their neighborhood. She would cross a street that led her to a trailhead, and then she'd ride up a dirt path through a valley that cut through the subdivision. It was settled land, but with a hint of wildness. Coyotes sometimes made appearances, and of late there had been mountain lion warnings posted on the trailheads. He'd advised her to go a different route, but she'd said she wouldn't be frightened away.

In the driveway Henderson saw the way it would unfold. There would be months to go yet. They'd seek out counseling. But he knew one day she'd be riding with another man. He'd be a whiz. He'd know all about fixing flats, could throw up a tent in a flash, chart their rides on a GPS.

In the driveway, his breath leaving him in a rush told Henderson how bad it was going to be. He stood in the driveway, taking in the houses across the street, the shingle roofs, the crabapple trees, taking in the glare of the evening sunlight, noting the fading paint of his neighbor's garage door and the slant of his own driveway, the way the concrete had settled and chipped over the years.

She'd climb from the valley, cross another street and a wooden bridge, and then ride around the lake. He saw her legs pumping, her face flushed with resolve, her breath hurried and then steadying as she hit her rhythm. He was proud of her. He urged her on.

THE NEXT TOWN OVER

SAMUELS WAS SITTING ON the couch in the den watching television, waiting for his wife to come home. He parted the curtain and saw that the snow was really coming down, a blizzard. She would be driving from the next town over and he hoped she would get home soon before the storm got even worse. They never referred to it as anything but the next town over, though it wasn't really a town, with no definable center; only a string of industrial buildings and shopping malls. She worked in a dentist's office. He liked calling her at work so he could hear her voice, but really, she could not talk long because she needed to book appointments. When she was away he had a curious sensation that he was lost in the house, wandering from room to room, looking for something but forgetting what he was looking for. Things seemed out of place, as if someone had moved them without notice. But as soon as she came home everything felt in its proper place again. He had asked her just that morning why she had to work in the next town over and she'd said that she would not have to work in the next town over if there wasn't the problem of bills. He had been retired for several years now and it was really up to her, she said, if they were going to keep the house and the electricity and things like that. "Sure," he said, "but do you really need to work in the next town over? Maybe you could work from home. A lot of people do."

She'd given a big sigh, slung her heavy bag over her shoulder, and headed out to her car in the garage. He followed her out so he could lift the garage door for her because the automatic door opener was broken. With the large, dark bag over her shoulder, she reminded him of a postal carrier from the days when the mailmen had walked their routes on foot. He missed seeing them, the way they'd give a friendly wave if they weren't warding off a dog or something. He'd given her his usual kiss, pleased that he could lift the garage door for her. Still, it was a long road to the next town over, past open space and fields, and if you broke down, who knew if someone might come along and murder you. He didn't think it was a good idea for her to work in the next town over.

The snow was really coming down hard and fast in big flakes. He sat back down on the couch. There was a report on the news about a man lost in a cave, but the lost man's sister said her brother was always disappearing. She implied that he might be a little off his rocker and might not be in the cave at all. The town sheriff was stumped. He didn't know whether to call off the search or not. Samuels wondered why anyone would go in a cave.

His cell phone rang on the coffee table in front of him. He hadn't much wanted the cell phone, but a few months before he'd taken a drive and ended up in the next town over and his wife insisted he have his own phone after that. It was his wife on the phone now and she was speaking urgently. It took him a moment to understand that she was telling him to turn down the television so that he could hear her. She always claimed he played the television so loudly that it was impossible for anyone to think in the house. He found the controller and lowered the volume. His wife kept talking, though he had set the phone down on the couch so her voice was muffled.

He picked the phone back up. "Okay. What's going on? Why aren't you home by now?"

"I've run off the road! I'm stuck. I can't see anything."

"That doesn't sound very good."

"Of *course* it doesn't sound very good!"

He had his eyes still on the screen, but he could only hear a murmur from the television. "There's a guy in a cave," Samuels said. "He's lost too, but they're not really sure if he's in there or not."

"*What?* What are you talking about?"

"I was watching the news. Where are you?"

"I don't know where I am. I was driving from the next town over! There's a whiteout blizzard and I can't see anything."

"We wouldn't be having this problem if you didn't work in the next town over. "

She said something and hung up. He tried to call back, but the call went to her voice messaging. Then the phone made beeping noises and he realized she was calling back.

Her voice was calmer now, still urgent but calmer, as if she were working on getting his full attention. She was like that. She would grip him by the arm and lean into his face and say, "I really need you to focus right now." She was always talking about *focus*, as if there were some problem with his focus.

In fact, she used the word now. "I need you to *focus*. I am lost. I am stuck in my car."

"Have you called 911?"

"I called them first. Then I called you. I wanted you to know that I would be late because I had run off the road."

"Well, I'd better come find you in case the 911 people can't."

"No, don't! You shouldn't drive. They'll find me."

She said something else, then the phone turned to static and he lost the connection.

The news report about the man lost in the cave was over. Now there were scenes of some people standing on the deck of a small boat. It was daylight in the scene and it was warmer there because the people on the deck were in shorts and T-shirts. They had orange life vests around their necks. Waves rocked the boat and another small boat was trying to maneuver in. Some rescuers were throwing out ropes that fell short of the other boat.

The phone rang again. Before she could tell him not to come, he said, "Stay where you are. I'll be right there."

He hung up and when the phone rang again he didn't answer. He glanced again at the television. Something had gone wrong and the rescue boat had backed away. The waves were getting worse. The situation looked hopeless.

As he went to the closet for his coat and boots he found himself thinking of an old girlfriend, a lifetime ago, when he was still a teenager. The girl's father had owned a motorboat and he would let them take it out. Samuels drove the motorboat and she skied behind. He'd turn his head and she'd wave with one hand. She looked pretty skiing behind the boat in her bikini, waving at him. In his memory he was wearing a baseball cap and he was looking back at her with a grin on his face. The boat went over some waves and she bounced up and down. The top of her swimsuit slipped off so that her breasts were exposed to the sky. She rode the waves, bare-breasted, tossing her head back, laughing into the spray of the water as he looked over his shoulder in wonder.

He found his coat and dug his boots out from deep in the front room closet. Faced with the prospect of going out in the cold, he became appreciative of how nice and warm it was in the house. He hadn't driven in a few weeks. He wondered where he would look for her. He supposed he would drive slowly and look for car tracks running off the road. Sure, the Subaru had good grooves in the tires. He'd look for tire tracks that were veering to the side. If he reached the next town over, he would know he'd gone too far and he would turn around. He would come back slowly and search from that direction. Why was a Subaru running off the road anyway? They were supposed to be good snow cars. He would call the dealer and complain. Maybe he could sue. Why not? Everybody was suing everybody; he might as well too.

His own tires weren't so great. He drove slowly, searching for the tire tracks, but the snow was coming down so heavy that it would probably cover up whatever tracks she had made. She was right about the whiteout. The road had disappeared. As he got farther from home he only knew he was somewhere on the way to the next town over. A tree sprang into his vision and he swung the wheel wildly to the right. What the hell was a tree doing in the road?

Just then the phone rang. He had set it on the passenger seat and as he reached for it his hand bumped it and it slid across the seat toward the door. He spread himself across the seat to grab it but came away empty-handed. The car went into a slide. As he righted himself he bumped over what felt like some logs in the road. He slammed into something and the airbag rushed at his chest. When the car settled he felt that he had gone lower into the earth, as if he were in a ditch of some sort. The engine was no longer running. He sat with the airbag pressed against his chest and nose. There was a curious smell which he couldn't quite place, maybe something like old canvas. His chest hurt and his nose was bleeding, but he thought he had come out of this pretty well, all things considered.

The phone had stopped ringing during his slide, but it was ringing again now. It sounded like it was below him, on the floorboard somewhere, but it was difficult to get to it with the airbag trapping him. On the left side of the front seat there was a lever that tilted the seat back. He pulled at the lever, pushed with his back against the seat, and slid away from the airbag. He twisted his body sideways and down and his hand grabbed the phone and he brought it up just before it stopped ringing.

"They found me!" his wife exclaimed. "They're getting me out of the car right now!"

"That's good," he said. "I'm happy to hear that."

"Where are you?"

"I'm not sure. Somewhere between our house and the next town over."

"*What!* Are you okay?"

"I've run off the road. I'm fine but my nose is bleeding a little."

"Oh my God!" He heard her talking to someone. "Stay there," she said. "We'll come find you."

"That's good," he said. "I'd like that."

"They want to speak to you. I'm going to put you on the phone to—" She started to say something else and he heard another voice but then he couldn't hear them at all. He kept listening and saying, "Hello? Hello? Is anyone there?" But the phone had gone dead. He remembered now that just this morning she had told him to charge it, but he had forgotten to.

But it was okay. They'd found her so there was really nothing to worry about. Pretty soon they'd find him and before long they'd be sitting on the couch watching television together like they did most nights. They liked to sit close, shoulders bumping, holding hands. They liked to watch the detective shows on Masterpiece Theater. They'd debate about who had done the crime, changing their minds as the show went along. They complained about not understanding the British accents, but that added to the fun. At the tense moments they squeezed their hands tightly together. He hoped that maybe tonight there would also be some more news about the man lost in the cave. He hoped the guy had made it out of there. It was getting a little cold, but that was okay. He'd just sit here and wait. She'd find him. She always did.

THE PROFESSOR'S MARCH

THE MORNING BEFORE THE madness began, the professor was teaching his literature class. What was unusual for him as he lectured on this sultry August day was how drastically his students changed from one minute to the next. One minute he looked out at thirty cynical, world-weary, mop-haired, slack-jawed juniors and the vitality drained from his voice, and in the next moment the professor felt his voice grow joyous as he addressed a class of astonishingly beautiful young men and women who were not only listening raptly but were dancing in the aisles to the rhythms of his voice. White and brown and black bodies, long-limbed and sinewy and magnificent, rocked away in the aisles, and the professor's face dripped sweat as the branches of the oak trees brushed against the classroom windows, rubbing their arms against the glass to urge the professor on. Then in the next moment the students stopped dancing in the aisles and were back in their seats, staring at the professor's dripping face and glancing nervously at each other. The professor did not know then if he was forming words or babbling in tongues; chuckling came at him like a wave from the back of the room, and the professor wiped his wet face, his heart rattling around like a rat in the cage of his chest. He felt his soaking face grow dark and he shivered wildly now, felt icy cold in the hot classroom, felt himself shrinking before the students. Then he became incredibly hot again, burning from his toes to his head, turning to a puddle of water before his students' eyes. He was lost and shouted in or into his own mind: *Calm down, you fool! It's only the LSD. Oh my God, why did I take the LSD Rebecca gave me?*

He took a deep breath and the students transformed again, looked calm and eager and interested, and he felt his cheeks gaining color, heard the resonance in his voice; he rallied before them, finished his lecture on "Prufrock" with a surge of energy. He spread his hands and bowed like a conductor. He indicated the door. Lecture over. My God, they looked happy now! He beamed at them. They looked so young, so pure, so innocent. They were happy little munchkins, calling cheerfully, See you, Dr. Robertson! Great class, Dr. Robertson!

A boy tugged at his sleeve. *Now*, about the pair of ragged claws scuttling across the floor in "Prufrock," the boy said . . . His face was mottled with red and gold colors. Thought creased his brow, and the professor could see the thought sitting weightily in the boy's mind like a wedge of apple pie. The professor could taste the thought; he had never tasted another person's thought before.

Well, it's like this, the professor said. It's really, don't you see, it's quite plain, it's like the claws are . . . well, they're scuttling, actually, is what they're doing. They're scuttling, and then they're . . . they're claws, and therefore they've a mind to scuttle . . . so you see, claws . . . claws scuttle . . . it's a known fact . . . you see . . .

No, I don't see, the boy said sullenly, and then, voice turning to a whine, I don't know why I can't see these things.

The professor patted the boy's shoulder. You will in time. Don't fear. He steered the boy toward the door. Not to worry. Leave it the English majors.

But I *am* an English major!

Plenty of time. Plenty of time. Pushing the boy to the door now, both hands on his back. Drink some beer, he called cheerfully. Meet a girl, forget the fucking claws.

The boy fell out the door as if sucked out by a current and the professor retreated to his desk, hands shaking as he tried to pack his briefcase. A voice behind him said loudly, What a knockoff! I thought you were losing it, for sure.

He whirled, papers falling off his desk. The she-devil herself! Raven-haired, slanted-nosed Rebecca. The pusher!

Why did you do this to me? he hissed. I'm going mad!

What did you expect, Professor? Be cool.

She grinned sharkily with crooked teeth. She was stout, attractive in a slovenly way, with a tie-dyed T-shirt and baggy camouflage pants. She was the best English major in the school and a horrible pain. The professor had always wanted her expelled.

Let's go to your office, she said. When I'm on acid, my body's on fire.

God, no. I don't consort with my students.

Bull. I've seen that Melissa in your office. I've seen the way you look at each other.

We haven't done anything wrong.

It's still an affair. You're in love. That's an affair. You're just too hung up to do anything.

She's a dear, sweet southern Baptist.

She'd drop her pants in a minute if you asked.

Don't speak that way. I'm repelled.

Her eyes turned hollow and dull. I'm stoned.

Oh, God. Why did you give me this?

He moaned. He recalled walking to work that morning. If it had not been so warm, so deliciously, wonderfully hot and steamy, and if he had not been spinning so in love with Melissa and the universe, so broken-heartedly in love with Melissa and the universe, this would not have happened.

Walking to school that morning before taking the LSD, walking down quiet, shady San Jacinto Street, a street of old two-story houses and giant oaks, he finds himself thinking portentously: Something will happen today. My life will change.

For so long he has been at the university; for so long. He had come to Texas in youthful middle age, with an honorary doctorate and books of acclaimed verse, a poet in his prime, and he had met a student and fallen in love and married and had a daughter and a crack-up—all in this city where he had never planned to stay. Oh, Austin, oh, Texas, I have grown old and you have snickered at my eastern civility. Something will happen today; I will change my life.

On this hot summer morning in 1966 the professor is walking to school, and amid his jumble of thoughts and feelings he takes a vast relief and pleasure in contemplating the stability of the university, the last unrockable bastion of civilization. True, the students were lumps of coal and the director would like to fire him, but there was a limit to the savagery for a man with tenure. When he went mad before, he was welcomed back. His colleagues did not mind, found him intriguing . . . less so as the years went by and the books declined, the poetry subsided to a whisper. But a man with a briefcase and an office to go to is a man with substance not easily robbed . . . And if they try to boot me out, I'll bar the fucking door! he thinks with sudden fierceness. I'll make my last stand!

In the world he could be violated, but his office, forever shaded by the oaks, was cool and quiet and peaceful, was his sanctuary . . . though the university was changing, the mood changing, the students growing more sullen, bitter, challenging, the manner of dress scandalous, their hair growing, body odor rising from the unwashed masses—not that the professor minded anarchy so much, when it wasn't directed at him. Students wanting their papers returned! Their papers *read!* The director wanting to see a syllabus! It was an outrage, an *outrage!*

On this hot summer morning, the Professor has not yet had his coffee so he is feeling drowsy and dazed after another night of drinking, and fighting with his wife, a woman twenty years younger. She was once, so long ago, so enamored of him, long, long ago, but has become so furious and unrelenting and bitter, and why they don't end it, God knows, but they go along and they fight, and what the professor finds most sad is that his wife actually believes there is some point to the fighting, believes they have a chance, but it is hard for him to fight with any true purpose.

The professor—a poet—is wearing a long-sleeved blue shirt and a dark tie, and he strolls down shady San Jacinto Street, a tall, thin man with longish white hair and a droopy white moustache. Carrying a briefcase on the languid summer morning, as he progresses toward the university, he feels himself joined by Youth. Youth emerge from the old houses and the apartment complexes around the school. Youth with their tie-dyed T-shirts and moppy Beatle's haircuts, on foot and on bikes, a horde of Youth marching on the university to attain the knowledge that will set them free. The professor—a figure of authority with his briefcase—thinks: So long, for so long . . . How long can I go on? He has been up all night, has finished a poem in the early hours, his first in over a year, and he is filled with an urge to cry out to the passing Youth: I have finished a poem this morning! I have the same longings and desires as you! Take my briefcase!

The professor sweats profusely as he walks down the street. His sweat-soaked shirt clings to his back. He has miscalculated. He should have worn a T-shirt like the students. There is not a spot on his shirt which has not soaked through. The sweat puddles on his buttocks and streams down his thighs.

He steps off the sidewalk and rests beneath a huge oak tree in the front lawn of one of the wooden houses. There's no real coolness beneath the tree, but he pauses and rests his cheek against the bark. A young couple bangs in and out of the house, carrying boxes from the front porch through a screened door into the house. The young man and woman raise irritable voices to each other and it is obvious to the professor that they love one another in a hostile sort of way. The young man has a wispy blond beard and a red bandana around his neck and the young woman wears a long frontier-style dress, and the professor feels a wave of intimacy sweep over him. He wishes this young couple well. They look angry, sure of themselves, and would-be wise. Be well, young couple, the professor thinks. You are the future. They spot him standing beneath the tree in their lawn and the professor smiles and waves and calls cheerfully, You are the future! They stand on their front porch with boxes in their arms; they frown at the sweating man in their yard.

The professor stumbles on. Nearing the campus, he stares up at the giant clock at the top of the tower. The campus tower rises over the city like a sentry, and the clock bell tolls the hour of ten. As he walks along the university drag the smell of coffee from a vending stand wafts over him. He purchases a large coffee with cream, goes to the curb, waits for the walk sign, and crosses Guadalupe Street with a drove of students. He is the only one in sight, he notes, who is carrying a briefcase. A sentence forms in his mind, a sentence which he wants suddenly to cry out, to shake these youths from their happy oblivion. He wants to cry out, I shall regain my rightful throne! The sentence startles him and makes him slosh coffee on his penny loafers.

In his office on the third floor he begins to dry. He leaves the door open a crack, blocked by a garbage can to keep the door from swinging wide open. He opens his briefcase and spreads books and papers before him, but the thought of reading any of the students' essays makes him queasy. Yearning for another cup of coffee, still trembling from the last potent cup, he goes down the corridor into the faculty lounge, quiet in this slack summer season, but Bob Franklin, the director, is just pouring himself a cup of coffee, and it is too late to back away.

Bob spots him and gives him a grimacing smile. The professor knows that Bob wonders from semester to semester how to get rid of him. Bob steps back from the coffee pot and allows the professor to sidle in to pour his own. Bob, hovering, breathes heavily through his nose, and the professor feels his eyes on his sweaty back. He longs to turn from the coffee pot and shout, I never said I was a real teacher!

He wasn't, really. It was just an insane thing he did to support his poetry. There had been complaints—papers not returned, disorganized lectures, texts ordered and never used.

Hey-ho, James, Bob says mock cheerfully. You missed the meeting yesterday, and you, not even a golfer. He wags his finger at the professor and makes tsking noises.

Ah, the meeting, the professor says, recalling that he had meant to go to the department meeting, sort of, but then he had started arguing with his wife; in fact, they had been arguing because he said that he was not going to the meeting and she had insisted that he go. She had this mad thing about him needing to protect his position, but he had actually *meant* to go before they'd started fighting about his not going, which was, he supposed, what he had really wanted after all, so that he really would not have to go. And he had not gone—and it was yet another small debit on the scorecard Bob was keeping.

I'm sorry, Bob, he says. I had a scold yesterday. I mean a cold

A cold? Bob says, as if astounded. A cold? A summer cold?

Well . . . yes.

Worst kind, Bob says. My God, man, take care of yourself. He grins malevolently. I don't know what we would do without you around here. We'd just be a bunch of dry, academic, good old boys. You give us flair, Jimbo. That's what you give us. You give us flair. We've got to be in it for the long haul, James. The long haul. You look sweaty.

The director follows him from the lounge, hand on his shoulder, kneading, and the professor wants to scream, Are you fucking my wife? He has seen them at the faculty parties, their heads together, the way she grows animated around Big Bob, the jocky, tennis-legged Milton man. Nothing worse than a jocky Milton man.

We should talk more, James. I hardly see you. I always enjoy our chats.

I know. I know. I get so busy. My work.

Yes, Bob sighs. Your work. You've got to remember the long haul, Jim. The long haul.

Bob's hand lingers on his shoulder, pats sadly. Have you lost weight, Jimmy?

Coffee in hand, the professor sits in his office on the third floor and stares out his window, past the lush oak branches, at the great stone library and the tower looming over the city. If he were to open his window and jump, he would likely not die but would land in a tree well and break his leg.

The day before, Melissa had broken his heart. True, they'd never really been lovers. That part of him had seemed dead until just yesterday.

Was it so strange that Melissa had reminded him of his daughter Jill? Or of the kind of woman Jill might grow into? True, she did not have Jill's intelligence or psychic toughness, but what she did have was a vast ability to believe in him, and a sensitivity which made her blue eyes mist over whenever the professor read poetry to the class. When the professor had returned a paper to her with a kind comment, she had come into his office, sat on the edge of a chair, smiling shyly, fidgeting with the bangs of her blonde hair, and said: You're the first teacher who's made poetry come alive for me.

He had heard similar compliments, but not so often in recent moons; in years of late he had slogged listlessly onward, reading the masterpieces as if they were the yellow pages. Occasionally he would rally before lapsing again into the banal.

At first he wanted to warn her to go away, to shout at her to leave him in peace. That was in the spring semester, and through the remainder of the semester he came to look forward to her office visits. He asked her questions about her life. She was twenty-two, from Lubbock; she had a fiancé; she was planning to go home and get married. Was she sure of this? the professor asked casually.

Oh, yes. Buddy was going into his father's ranching business. She'd go back home and tend to house and raise a family.

But didn't she want a career? Didn't she want to travel, perhaps, to leave Texas?

What was the point? she asked.

Did she like it so much then, the barbecues, the Lone Star beer, the hook 'em horns? God, no, she didn't care. She didn't like Lubbock all that much. Then why not leave? Oh, she had her family there, she had her life; everybody had a life to live—that was enough. Lubbock was . . . well . . . home . . . and it was her life, and it was enough.

But what do you really *want*? the professor asked one day.

Oh, to make Buddy happy. To make my family happy.

Well, sure, the professor said. To make people happy is a very fine thing. But what do *you* want? What would make *you* happy?

What would make *me* happy is to make *them* happy.

The professor frowned. That is very dangerous thinking.

She laughed, her delightful ranch-girl, hearty laugh. *Dangerous?* she said shrilly.

Oh, Texas girl! He wanted to reach out and hold her. You are all of Texas sitting in my office, you rangy blonde.

A semester is a lifetime, though, and later in the spring she didn't want to just answer questions but to ask them. He told her bits about himself, his past, and he felt as if he were talking about a third party, an eager young man who had set out years before to claim his rightful throne. They talked through the spring, fifteen minutes one day, half an hour the next, an hour one day, and he saw that she was nothing like his daughter, really, except in her willingness to listen to him, to make him feel like he still had important things to say, was not a dry, old windbag. She began to remind him of his wife, not as she was now but in their early days when she, too, had been his student. He'd been different then, young and vibrant and making a name for himself. Now he played a different role—older, possessed of a certain sad knowing. His wife had made the mistake of thinking she was hooking onto a rising star; Melissa was making the mistake of thinking she could stop the descent of a falling one.

By May she was falling in love with him. Her glances in the

classroom and in his office were long and heavy. And at times as she stared at him, her eyes misting over, he wanted to cry: Run! Save yourself! Flee back to Lubbock! Marry Buddy quickly! Run, my Texas belle! Run back to the 4-H club, to the cows; run back to the sagebrush, the sand, the mesquite; watch sunrises and sunsets and measure out the days of your life. It is encugh. Let what is be enough.

When the spring semester was over she stayed in Austin for summer school, and though she was no longer in his class she continued to visit him in his office. She was confused now, and she was a young woman who had not often been confused because she'd had the good sense not to want too much.

And the professor began to resent her now because he saw that she wanted more than to sit in his office and allow him to be distantly, safely in love with her. Now she wanted something from him, something he no longer had to give, and for this he resented her.

His greatest pleasure, she did not understand, was in her leaving. Their chats, in fact, now bored him. The moment of pleasure was when her tall, long, raw-boned body pushed up from her chair, when she unslung her purse from the chair and slid the strap over her arm—left bare by her sleeveless sundress, revealed as tanned and lean and muscular—and settled it on her shoulder. The moment of pleasure came each day when she paused at the door and they looked at each other and they wondered if this was the day. Was this the day they would fall into each other's arms? Was this the day he would draw her back into the office and crash with her to his disorderly desk? And at the last moment their eyes would flicker away from each other's and he'd send her off with some banality: Good luck with the chem test! Going out the door, she'd call breezily, since it was not the day after all: Thanks again for your time!

Not at all! Not at all!

He'd close the door softly behind her and fall into his chair and swivel toward the window, savoring the last whiffs of her perfume as he stared out at the grassy mall where the students lounged, half-clothed, sleepy and horny and happy.

Go back, Melissa. Back to your Buddy, your ranch, your bingo games and barbecues, back to your days of dust and dirt and sagebrush.

In the last days, though, she was pressuring him. As she stood and slipped her purse over her shoulder, her long, lean body had taken on a squared-off look. She bit her lip and frowned and waited, and the professor cringed inside, his shoulders rigid, the breath high in his chest. Texas awaited him, stood squared-off, raw, sassy, and bold. Texas could not wait to grab his longish white hair and pull his face down to her throat and whisper: Fill me with poetry, make me your metaphor, mount me with madness.

Now, as he sent her away, his words sounded hollow and mincing: Good luck with your anatomy test!

And out she'd go, surly, breathing huffily.

And then the day before, finally, she stood so long, waited so long, leveled her eyes so long, sighed so heavily, that he took a step forward and reached out. He caught himself, but she'd seen his look and her hand snaked out and captured his wrist. She pulled his tall, skinny body to her and kissed him hard on the lips.

He moaned, Oh, Melissa, and put his hands on her breasts, and all of it came back to him, the neglected feelings of desire and lust. He tried to encircle her with his arms and she stiff-armed him in the chest. Whoa now, she said, backing away.

She was breathing hard. I just wanted to tell you I'm leaving school. I'm going back to Lubbock to marry Buddy.

Dizzy, heart thudding, he watched her back toward the office door. You're a great man and I won't forget you. I want to thank you for opening my eyes to a whole 'nother world. But I'm going back to Lubbock now.

She was gone, out the door, and the professor sank into his chair and stared out the window at the soft, hot afternoon. He put his fingers together and played: Here is the church, here is the steeple, look inside and here are all the people.

That was yesterday, and this morning, defenses weakened, the professor had dropped acid.

If he had not been so weakened by Melissa's rejection and by the heat, and if he had not spiraled so high on his coffee rush and plummeted so shakily, hands trembling, stomach gurgling, he would have been able to resist Rebecca when she offered him the clear little chip.

Rebecca was the other student who visited him in his office. She had a chubby, sulking face and black, frizzy hair, and when she talked one could see silver gleaming in her teeth. When Rebecca visited she propped her combat boots atop his desk and picked itchily at her dirty jeans. She was the brightest student in the department and she frightened him. She had told him she was aware that he didn't plan his lectures, that most of what he said was off the wall. But she didn't mind, she told him. He was pretty cool in an obsolete way.

This morning she'd propped her boots on his desk as usual. Have you ever gotten high? she asked.

A few times. I didn't like it. It gave me rapid heartbeats.

Just pot? That's all you tried?

He nodded.

What about acid?

Madness. Not interested. Spend a day in my household if you want a hallucinatory experience.

You call yourself a poet and you haven't even tried acid. Phony. You don't know anything about life; how can you write about it?

He stared at the smirking girl and wanted to knock her combat boots off his desk. Rebecca, you're not wanted in my office anymore.

She slid her boots off his desk. Don't you even want to know what it looks like?

My God, do you have some on you? Lower your voice.

Don't you give a damn about anything new? Don't you give a damn about *living*? Are you completely *dead*?

Shut up. Let me see what it looks like.

From her jeans pocket she extracted a small tin aspirin container. She opened the lid and held the tin in her palm as the professor stared inside at what looked like an empty container.

I don't see anything.

Look closer. It's clear. It's called windowpane.

He stared intently, still not seeing, and then from the white metal background two tiny, transparent chips emerged. They looked like clear bits of glass, perfectly squared. They looked, somehow, incredibly pure and beautiful. There was a quality about the lovely chips that the professor found almost religious, as if they should be served in a place of sanctuary.

That's it? That's LSD?

The purest kind.

He checked his watch. I have to teach in five minutes.

It takes a while to work. You probably won't even feel anything until after class.

Oh, God. Why am I even talking to you?

Why do you think people don't read your work anymore? You're obsolete. You're a Victorian living in a new world.

A savage, uncivilized new world which I want no part of. I want the city divided into two camps—the brutes and Visigoths like yourself kept on one side of town, the civilized—

The dead kept on the other.

There is a certain proclivity here, he said, his voice trembling angrily. Do you understand that? There is a certain proclivity. You know my history.

So maybe what you *need* is another fucking crack-up! It's now or never, Professor. This moment, right here. Play it safe or screw your courage to the sticking point. Are you going to be a poet of the new world or are you going to keep writing drivel about fucking roses? About the only place you're ever read anymore is in the nursing homes.

That's it. You're expelled. You're out of this university.

You're out of this university except in name alone. She shrugged, wet her fingertip with her tongue, and touched one of the chips. She raised her fingertip to her mouth, sucked and swallowed.

You did it, he said, amazed. You violated my office. I'm going to the dean. I'll have you shackled.

Now or never.

Damn you. He imitated the motion she had made, wetting his fingertip and touching it to the clear chip, raising his fingertip to his lips, sucking, and swallowing.

Did I get it down? I think it's caught in my teeth.

You did fine, Professor. Welcome to the sixties. She laughed dreamily. Ta-ta. See you in class.

He'd barely gotten through class with the students gyrating and rocking around in the aisles like happy savages, and now here was evil, silver-toothed Rebecca standing beside his desk after class. Her mouth was split open in a great, wicked leer. He wanted to shake her, and to his surprise he discovered he *was* shaking her. She was staring at him now, wide-eyed and terrified as he shook her and demanded: How long does this last?

Only twelve hours, she said, though you may feel some residual effects.

Oh, God, the professor moaned. Why did you poison me?

They left the classroom and the English building together and there was nothing disturbing the professor quite so much as the sensation that he was sweating out white plastic from the pores of his face. He kept rubbing a hand across his face, wiping off white plastic sweat with his palm. He asked Rebecca over and over: How do I look? Do I look all right? Do I have plastic on my face?

What? she screamed at him, her purple lips twisting monstrously. What is *wrong* with you? Are you *fucked up*?

Shoes clicking on the stone courtyard, they walked huddled shoulder to shoulder between the library and botany building. They passed a statue of a Greek in a toga and the professor was certain he'd seen the statue in his class that morning; the statue had stood in the back of the room wearing a querulous expression as the professor had lectured on "Prufrock." He felt the statue's eyes follow his progress, and now he was aware that all the students in the courtyard were turning their heads to look at him. Rebecca's face bobbed in close to his, her nose hooked and enormous, her lips purple and garish. Stop knocking off! she snarled.

The professor saw that he was doomed, and he had always thought that a doomed man should make some final graceful gesture, so he paused, briefcase in hand, and pirouetted, once and then again, and in a nearby fountain that Lady Bird Johnson had built to beautify the campus he saw the Greek in toga playing the violin. Rebecca's face bobbed in, teeth bared, her mouth foaming: Knock-off! The Greek slipped beneath the water and the professor marched on.

Rebecca led him to a café on the drag, just across from the university. They drank Cokes and the professor felt like the soda was burning the lining of his mouth and stomach. In the wooden booth Rebecca was again warning him not to be a knock-off. Then she pushed away from the table and disappeared toward the back of the café, in the direction of the phone and the restrooms.

He was alone in the booth and the people in the café stared at him as he sweated white plastic, and he realized that a person could not be sure if what he thought was occurring was really occurring or if he was only imagining that it was occurring, and he knew that this was the kind of thinking that had landed him in the madhouse. He was not sure now if he really had dropped acid that morning or if he had only imagined that he'd taken it, and he was not sure now if he had really walked across the campus with Rebecca or if he had come into this café alone, and the most frightening thing of all was his uncertainty about whether he was really sitting in this booth at all.

How did he know that he wasn't only imagining sitting in the booth? How did he know that he wasn't really somewhere else entirely, doing something that did not even remotely resemble sitting in a booth? How did he know that he wasn't actually in some terrible predicament? Perhaps he was actually dying right now, lying in the street crushed beneath a car's wheels, and this invented day was only his mind's kind way of trying to spare him from this awful truth. As if to verify the hypothesis, pain seared through his stomach and ribs. Tears ran down his face, and when the hand touched his wrist and the voice spoke softly, he looked blurrily up into the face of his daughter, who was now sitting across from him in the booth. He blinked at the image before him. His daughter was glowing, a lovely, soft yellow light encircling her; she was smiling and the professor understood then that sanctuary was not a matter of place but of person. Jill, his lovely daughter he called Craggly, was his sanctuary.

Craggly, is it really you? he spoke, thinking blissfully that there really was an afterlife, for here he was communicating with his daughter on the spirit level. Craggly, listen, I've been run over. Tell your mother not to bother about my supper.

What in the hell are you talking about? a rough voice asked. He saw the way his yellow-glowing daughter scooted gently over on the wooden seat to make room for broad-assed Rebecca. He was proud of her. A certain measure of grace was necessary when dealing with savages, even intellectual ones.

You knock-off, Rebecca snarled, garish purple lips moving and spitting out the words seconds after the first movement of her mouth. Here. She pushed a dish of vanilla ice cream with chocolate syrup at him. Eat this. Who were you talking to?

He exchanged a look with Craggly, who cautioned him not to mention her presence. I can't tell if I'm sitting here, the professor said.

Where are you, then?

I may have been run over by a car.

God. I don't know why I bothered to give you acid. It's wasted on you.

I have to call my wife.

Now that would be really stupid.

Call my wife. There's a certain proclivity here.

Why didn't you tell me you couldn't handle drugs? she asked sourly, pushing away from the booth and heading for the back of the restaurant.

From the booth he watched as she talked on the phone. His daughter held his hand again and he discovered that by breathing very low in his stomach and by repeating over and over the words *everything is okay, everyone is happy, everything is okay, everyone is happy* he could calm himself. He felt his daughter's soothing glow spread to his own body. Now the two of them were in the booth glowing blissfully away. The people at the other tables had been suspicious of him for sweating white plastic out of his face, but now he was able to beam glowing light at them and they were relaxing and smiling.

The professor knew what he must do now. He must return to the English building and reclaim his rightful throne. He must let his glow spread through the stale corridors, purify the years of waste and neglect and abuse; he must let his glow creep under the director's door, catch him unawares like a sudden scent of perfume, the director rising from his chair, pronouncing, My God, we've all been doing it wrong around here! The professor spreading warmth, love, honesty throughout the English building, not only ending forever but correcting, transforming all the wretched years of subtle savagery.

Rebecca was back. Your wife wasn't home, and if I were you— why are you smiling like that? You look insane!

I'm going to the English building. I've got to spread my glow.

I hate you. I wish I'd never gotten you stoned. You're the sickest person I've ever known.

Peace.

Eat shit!

I must go.

Recrossing Guadalupe Street, he proudly, serenely carried his briefcase, and with his other hand held the hand of his daughter, who trotted alongside him. Rebecca was frightened and was arguing that he must not go back to the English building. He found her agitated and paranoid and he wished that she would disappear and let him go about his business.

Yards in front of him a student fell, dropped abruptly and lay still on the stone courtyard, and moments later, as if someone had tapped an ice pick into the side of his head, his blood streamed out. The professor heard popping sounds and there was a still moment in the courtyard when no one moved, when scores of people stood looking about in amazement—there was a perfectly long, still moment and then the professor followed the lifting heads and he, too, saw the puffs of white smoke from the tower and all at once everyone was screaming and running and Rebecca screamed in his ear, *Run! It's happening!* and then she was running with the others. Jill, too, was suddenly gone. To the side of him another boy fell, but the boy was clutching his shoulder and screaming as the bullets whizzed through the air and ricocheted off the pavement. The professor took the wounded boy under the armpits. He knew now the director was shooting from up in the tower; the director had learned of his march to reclaim his rightful throne.

Jill reappeared, beckoning with a glowing hand toward a clump of bushes, and he dragged the wounded boy into cover in the bushes. He was starting back for another wounded boy when he felt the wind in his hair, felt something catch at the side of his head, and then the professor was toppling over. He fell beside the boy and lay there unmoving for a moment as the bullets whizzed around them. He had the sense that something was wrong with him, very wrong. But Jill urged him once again toward the bushes, and he crawled, dragging the boy, until they were both in cover. Rebecca was looming over him, pressing her hands to the side of his head. Now you're *wounded*, you fucking idiot! she screamed.

The word reverberated in his ears, *wounded wounded wounded wounded*, filled his ears, his mind, *wounded wounded wounded*

wounded. The word pulsed and echoed. Faces loomed over him, faded, until all he could see was Jill's glowing, yellow face above him.

The last thought before he lost consciousness was that he did not know if he was really lying there; he did not know if he was already dead; time had come unstuck, lost its order, and wasn't it actually perhaps still the morning and wasn't he walking to school through the sultry heat, pouring sweat out his back, his neck, his thighs, and didn't he have a class to teach and when he arrived at the school wouldn't he still have all this to look forward to, and wouldn't it all keep happening over and over, the same reel playing in endless repetition, the professor walking down quiet, shady San Jacinto street, the professor in his office meeting Rebecca, teaching his class, the students rocking away in the aisles, the walk across campus, the Greek playing the violin in the fountain, the café, his glowing daughter in the booth, the march on the English building, the director shooting at him from the tower.

When he woke in the night in the hospital, for a time there was nothing. He did not know his name, who he was, or where he had come from. He sensed two things only: that someone had saved him, though it would be another sleep and waking before he would recall the glowing figure of his daughter, and that he had lost something. He wracked his brain in the darkness of the hospital room. He had been carrying something, something vital and important. And this, too, would take another sleeping and waking, to recall his briefcase, and when memory came back to him he would know that the old order was ruined, that the last thin defense had been penetrated. The last civilized bastion had fallen.

But in the hospital room that night he was still without memory. His head hurt and when he raised his hand he felt bandages. He had a keyed-up feeling, a pounding in his chest, and he knew he must rise and try to find this important thing he had been carrying. He rolled out of bed, dragging tubes, and a shape emerged from the darkness, sat bolt upright in a chair and rose and grabbed him—a woman, short, sturdy, with strong fingers. He knew, somehow, that he knew her, that she was closely related to him. In fact, he suspected that she was his wife, though he could recall nothing else about their relationship.

Get back in bed, James. I'll call the nurse.

Certainly. Certainly, dear.

He did not want to admit that he had not known his name was James. He would play along. The woman seemed stern and fierce, but he had a sense that she was not surprised, that she was used to handling him.

Darling, help me, he whispered.

I always do. Get back in bed.

As her strong hands eased him back into the vast whiteness, he understood clearly then, in a way that hurt him to the bone, that the woman loved him, and that he had made her life an unhappy one.